Welcome to this month's [illegible] Harlequin Presents!
At this festive time of year, why not bring some extra
sparkle and passion to your life by relaxing with our
brilliant books! For all of you who've been dying to read
the next installment of THE ROYAL HOUSE OF NIROLI,
the time has come! Robyn Donald continues the series with
The Prince's Forbidden Virgin, where Rosa and Max
struggle with their mutual—but dangerous—desire, until
the truth about a scandal from the past may set them free.

Also this month, Julia James brings you *Bedded, or Wedded?*
Lissa's life has too many complications, but she just
can't resist ruthless Xavier's dark, lethal sexuality.
In *The Greek Tycoon's Pregnant Wife* by Anne Mather,
Demetri needs an heir, but before he divorces Jane, he'll
make love to her one last time. In *The Demetrios Bridal
Bargain* by Kim Lawrence, Mathieu wants a wife of
convenience, and taming wild Rose into the marital
bed will be his pleasure! Sharon Kendrick brings you
Italian Boss, Housekeeper Bride, where Raffaele
chooses his mousy housekeeper, Natasha, to be his
pretend fiancée! If you need some help getting in the
holiday mood, be sure not to miss the next two books!
In *The Italian Billionaire's Christmas Miracle* by
Catherine Spencer, Domenico knows unworldly Arlene isn't
mistress material, but might she be suitable as his wife? And
in *His Christmas Bride* by Helen Brooks, Zak is determined
to claim vulnerable Blossom as his bride—by Christmas!
Finally, fabulous new author Jennie Lucas brings you
The Greek Billionaire's Baby Revenge, in which Nikos is
furious when he discovers Anna's taken his son, so he vows
to possess Anna and make her learn who's boss! Happy
reading, and happy holidays from Harlequin Presents!

RUTHLESS

Men who can't be tamed...or so they think!

If you love strong, commanding men,
you'll love this miniseries.

Meet the guy who breaks the rules to get
exactly what he wants, because he is...

HARD-EDGED & HANDSOME
He's the man who's impossible to resist.

RICH & RAKISH
He's got everything—and needs nobody...
until he meets one woman.

He's RUTHLESS!
In his pursuit of passion; in his world
the winner takes all!

Brought to you by your favorite
Harlequin Presents® authors!

Julia James

BEDDED, OR WEDDED?

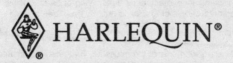

TORONTO • NEW YORK • LONDON
AMSTERDAM • PARIS • SYDNEY • HAMBURG
STOCKHOLM • ATHENS • TOKYO • MILAN • MADRID
PRAGUE • WARSAW • BUDAPEST • AUCKLAND

ISBN-13: 978-0-373-12684 2
ISBN-10:   0-373-12684-0

BEDDED, OR WEDDED?

First North American Publication 2007.

This edition published by arrangement with Harlequin Books S.A.

® and TM are trademarks of the publisher. Trademarks indicated with ® are registered in the United States Patent and Trademark Office, the Canadian Trade Marks Office and in other countries.

www.eHarlequin.com

Printed in U.S.A.

All about the author...
Julia James

JULIA JAMES lives in England with her family.
Harlequin® novels were the first "grown-up" books
she read as a teenager, along with the works of
Georgette Heyer and Daphne du Maurier, and she's
been reading them ever since. Julia adores the British
countryside in all its seasons, and is fascinated by all
things historical, from castles to cottages. She also has a
special love for the Mediterranean, which she believes
to be the most perfect landscape after England. She
considers both ideal settings for romance stories! Since
becoming a romance writer, she has, she says, had the
great good fortune to start discovering the Caribbean
as well, and she is happy to report that those magical,
beautiful islands are also ideal settings for romance
stories. "One of the best things about writing romance
is that it gives you a great excuse to take holidays in
fabulous places," says Julia. "All in the name of research,
of course!"

Her first stab at novel-writing was Regency romances.
"But, alas, no one wanted to publish them," she says.
She put her writing aside until her family commitments
were clear, and then renewed her love affair with
contemporary romances. "My writing partner and I
made a pact not to give up until we were published—
and we both succeeded! Natasha Oakley writes for
Mills & Boon® Romance™, and we faithfully read each
other's works-in-progress and give each other a lot of
free advice and encouragement."

When not writing, Julia enjoys walking, gardening,
needlework, baking "extremely gooey chocolate cakes"
and trying to stay fit!

CHAPTER ONE

XAVIER LAURAN, chief executive, chairman and majority share-holder of the XeL luxury goods company, whose ornate logo graced so many of the expensive possessions of the rich and famous, scanned down the e-mails on his desktop PC. The words of Armand's e-mail from London leapt from the screen in front of him.

...she's the woman of my dreams, Xav—she doesn't know it yet, but I'm going to marry her!

Xavier's jaw tightened. For a moment he brooded darkly, staring out over the darkening Paris skyline, the Arc de Triomphe visible from the windows of the XeL headquarters, overlooking the Place d'Etoiles. He should, right now, be leaving his office and going back to his apartment to change, ready to escort Madeline to the opera—and thereafter back to her apartment for their usual mutually enjoyable end to the evening. The arrangement suited him. Madeline de Cerasse, like all the women he selected for his leisure hours, knew what he wanted from a relationship and provided him with it—sophisticated companionship at the many social events his position required him to attend, and then, in private, equally sophisticated pleasures of an intimate nature. Physically intimate. Emotional intimacy was something Xavier neither sought nor desired. He was not, he knew with candid self-awareness, someone who let his heart rule his head.

Unlike his brother.

Xavier's expression darkened. Armand always let his heart rule his head—and the last time it had happened it had been a disaster. With complete lack of judgement, he had fallen into the clutches of a woman who had taken unscrupulous advantage of his good heart, deviously trotting out some rubbish about having to keep her frail grandmother in an expensive nursing home, as well as wringing his heart with tales about the charity for African orphans she'd claimed to work for. Armand had responded generously—until Xavier, with his habitual protectiveness of his younger brother, had had the woman checked out. Only to discover she had been lying through her teeth in order to win Armand's sympathy and money for herself.

Armand had been duly disillusioned. But his faith in the general goodness of people—and especially women—was undiminished. And now he was talking about marriage.

To whom? Who was this 'woman of his dreams'? Armand had said nothing about who his intended bride was. Swiftly Xavier scanned the remaining lines of the e-mail.

This time I'm being cautious, Xav, the way you like me to be. She doesn't even know that I've anything to do with you or XeL—I deliberately haven't told her. I want it to be a wonderful surprise!

But any initial relief that Armand was showing signs of thinking with his head dissolved into deepest foreboding as he finished the e-mail.

I know there will be problems, but I don't care if she isn't the ideal bride you think I should have—I love her and that has to be enough...

Grimly, Xavier stared at the screen. This was not good—not good at all. Armand was admitting upfront there would be problems and that his bride was not ideal.

Yet he was still talking about marriage.

Alarm speared through Xavier. If this woman turned out as disastrously as the last one had, extricating his brother would be far more difficult if he married her.

And expensive, too—Armand was not the type to consider a pre-nup. OK, so Armand was only his half brother, and had therefore not inherited the company founded by Xavier's grandfather, another Xavier Lauran. A company which was riding high—and very lucratively—as one of the world's most recognisable global brands of luxury goods. The exclusive XeL logo giving cachet and social status to anyone possessing any of the myriad extortionately expensive items, from watches to suitcases, which the company produced. But not only was Armand a very highly paid director of XeL, but his father, Lucian Becaud, whom Xavier's mother had married after her early widowing when Xavier was a small child, was comfortably wealthy in his own right. Armand would be a rich catch for any woman in search of a moneyed husband.

Was that what Armand's intended bride was? Armand clearly did not think so. The final lines of his e-mail were adamant.

Xav—this time around, trust me. I know what I'm doing, and you can't change my mind. Please don't interfere this time—it's too important to me.

Xavier sighed harshly. He wanted to trust Armand—but what if his brother were wrong? What if another unscrupulous woman had succeeded in blinding him to her true nature? There would be heart-break for his brother down the line—not to mention the expense of an acrimonious divorce and the distress to Armand's parents.

No, he could not take the risk. Not with his own brother's happiness. He needed to find out who this woman was, and whether his brother was safe with her. Reluctantly, but with grim determination, he reached for the phone on his desk. He would make some discreet enquiries. The company's security team answered to him alone—and if he required them to keep his brother under surveillance for a short while they would simply assume it was for Armand's protection. Not that his movements might reveal the identity of this woman so worryingly far from being 'the ideal bride', whom he'd already conceded would come with 'problems'.

As he waited for his head of security to answer, Xavier could feel the thoughts forming in his mind. *Maybe he was overreacting. Worrying unnecessarily.*

He hoped so—he really hoped so.

But within twenty-four hours he knew that his hopes had been in vain. As he gazed grimly down at the dossier in front of him, freshly delivered by his security team, he knew that without a doubt there was definitely—very definitely—a problem.

Armand had been right—this girl was not 'the ideal bride'. Xavier's mouth thinned. But then who in their right mind would think that of a girl who worked as a hostess in a Soho casino?

That she was just that was indisputable. Armand had been followed leaving the London HQ of XeL at the end of the working day, and taking a taxi to a part of South London no one would live in by choice. There, he had been granted entry to a ground-floor flat in a rundown tenement block by a young woman who had welcomed him warmly. He had stayed until mid-evening, when the woman had seen him out. Whereupon Armand had embraced her on the doorstep and spoken earnestly to her. The young woman had then been kept under surveillance herself, and within half an hour had left the flat. She had been followed to Soho, to the casino named in the dossier, where enquiries had confirmed she was employed as a hostess.

Xavier dropped the baldly written report down on his desk. His stomach clenched. *This* was the woman Armand intended to marry? To bring home to his family, be the mother of his children?

Was he completely mad?

With a harsh intake of breath, he ripped open the envelope marked with a single name: Lissa Stephens.

Then he slid out a photo, and stared at it. Just what was it that Lissa Stephens possessed by way of charms to entrap his brother?

As he stared, Xavier's disbelief mounted. As did his bleak dismay. The girl had been photographed at the casino, presumably covertly, by one of his security team's agents. She could hardly have looked worse.

Blonde, backcombed hair, make-up a centimetre thick, a scarlet slash of a mouth and a skimpy satin low-cut dress. Crudely…blatantly…displayed.

What the hell did Armand see in her?

Revulsion shot through him. How could Armand possibly want a woman like that?

Xavier's eyes narrowed. Did his brother even know she was a casino hostess in London's infamous red light district, Soho? He felt the blood run cold in his veins. And was that revelation merely the tip of the iceberg?

He could feel his own revulsion mount in him, and with deliberate effort he contained it. It was essential—to his brother's happiness, and his parents'—that the right call be made on this Lissa Stephens. Reason demanded that there was a chance—however slim—that appearances were deceptive. Reason, not emotion.

Could it possibly be that the girl was not as bad as she looked?

His eyes went to the photo again. Disbelief shot through him—could this really be the woman his brother wanted to *marry?* The very thought of Armand marrying such a female, presenting her to their mother, his father, seeing her making herself at home in the beautiful Riviera villa in Menton, watching his brother be first besotted and then bitterly disillusioned, was anathema.

He looked down at the two-dimensional image of Lissa Stephens, trying to see beyond it. He could read nothing from her expression, her make-up was like a mask, but one aspect of her appearance she could not mask.

Her eyes.

They were hard. The eyes of a woman who would see his brother's good heart as a weakness to be taken advantage of. Armand's words sounded in his mind.

I know what I'm doing...

Did he? Or did he just think he did—as he had before, until he'd had the truth presented to him? A harsh, heavy sigh escaped Xavier. He couldn't take that risk. If the woman that Armand wanted to marry was what she looked to be, then he had to protect him from her.

But how to know that?

Slowly, he got to his feet and walked across the large office, with its beautiful mouldings and high ceilings, and gazed out of the wide windows. The never-ending swirl of traffic around the Arc de Triomphe blurred before his eyes.

He had not steered XeL to the pinnacle it now stood upon without being able to make good judgements, shrewd decisions. His cool, analytical mind was capable of assessing anything from the optimum time to launch a new range of goods in any particular line to which overseas markets would prove the most profitable in the near to mid-term, and which of the many women of his acquaintance eager to become his next *chère amie* he would choose.

Now, faced with what could well be the debacle of a *mésal-*

liance that would devastate his brother and appal his mother and stepfather, Xavier knew he must apply the same detached, rational assessment to Armand's situation. And in the end, for something this important, this crucial to his brother's happiness and his family's peace of mind, a bare investigative report and a photo were not enough. Nowhere near enough.

He would have to check her out. See for himself. Judge her for himself.

It was a task that had to be done. He might not want to do it, but he must. Whatever was required he would do.

His brother deserved no less.

As for Lissa Stephens… His eyes darkened to slate. Well, he would find out, personally, just exactly what it was she deserved. His brother as her husband—or something quite different.

CHAPTER TWO

LISSA surreptitiously smothered a yawn, then, by force of will, turned it into a smile and murmured some facile pleasantry to the two men sitting at the table with her. Tiredness washed over her in a debilitating wave. Dear God, when would she get enough sleep ever again? She knew she had to be grateful for this job—even though what she was doing was demeaning, soul-destroying, morally dubious and grated on every last shred of sensibility in her.

Her face hardened momentarily. Well, tough. She needed the money. She needed it badly. Badly enough to put in a day's secretarial work temping in the City, and then work here until the early hours. The only other night job would have been cleaning—and it simply didn't pay as well.

Money, she thought grimly. It just came right back down to that—no escape. She needed money. She needed to earn as much as she could, in as short a time as she could, and that was all there was to it. No escape, no let up. And none likely, either.

Or was there? Through her weariness of body and spirit, a familiar, dangerously alluring thought flickered.

Armand.

Armand and his money could make it all happen so, so quickly. For just a few tantalising moments she allowed herself the luxury of daydreaming—how easy everything would be.

No—she must not allow herself to think about that. To allow herself hope. He had been out of touch for several days now, and she simply had to allow for the very real possibility that she had only been imagining his interest. That whatever hopes he had left behind, he was just not coming back.

Her throat tightened—disappointment was cruel, but she had always had to face the possibility that his interest was only temporary, a novelty. She could not, must not, rely on it. Rely on him. She stiffened her spine—it was pointless to expect anyone to wave a magic wand and make everything miraculously better.

She made herself focus on the two businessmen. At least they were engaged in talking to each other now—something about sales figures—rather than paying attention to her. Her gaze wandered off again.

And halted in mid-sweep.

Someone had just entered the casino's bar area. Someone who, she could instantly see, stood out from the rest of the punters here the same way a racehorse stood out from a field of hacks. Lissa's eyes widened.

He should be somewhere seriously flash—Monte Carlo, Marbella, one of the top West End hotels like the Ritz or the Savoy.

It was his whole appearance—from the superbly cut tuxedo that must have been handmade to sit so perfectly on his body, to the glint of gold at his pristine white cuffs and the razored perfection of his haircut.

And the tan. Nothing artificial or overdone about his skin tone—his was the real thing. Part nature, part thanks to a Riviera lifestyle.

He looked—rich. Seriously rich. Her stomach gave a little skip. The way Armand did sometimes. With a casual, inbred elegance that could never be put on. That you had to be raised with to show it the way Armand and this guy did.

He had something else in common with Armand—he wasn't English. That was obvious. No Englishman had the kind of svelte elegance that fitted like a smooth, flawless glove over bone-deep masculinity. But although Armand, too, possessed those rich continental looks, there was a very clear distinction between him and this man.

Armand's face was pleasant-looking, with an open, friendly expression. The man who had just walked in—her stomach gave a skip that turned into a full-scale 360 degree flip—was the most devastating male she'd ever set eyes on.

It was the tall, lean body, the tanned, planed face with its thin blade of a nose, the high cheekbones, perfectly contoured jaw-line, sculpted mouth. And the eyes. Dark, shadowed, with etched eyebrows that just for a moment gave the set of his face a satur-nine expression.

Her stomach flipped again, and she could feel a sudden pulse at her throat. She tried to subdue it. She'd seen handsome men before. Why make such a fuss over this one?

The answer came to her. Because she'd never seen a man like this before, that's why.

The pulse beat at her throat again.

Annoyed with herself now, she made to pull her eyes away. What on earth did it matter that she'd never seen a man as devas-tating as that before? He was a punter, that was all. And, as a punter, the only interest anyone working here in the casino would have in him was in parting him from as much money as they could.

Even as the thought formed in her mind she saw the casino manager gliding forward. His eyes must be glinting, Lissa thought, at the prospect of such a fat fish arriving in his net. Through lowered lashes she watched the byplay of the manager fawning on the new arrival. Then, with a swift, searching glance around the bar, he beckoned for a hostess. The best in the house. Lissa was not surprised. Tanya was a voluptuous Slavic blonde, and she sashayed towards the newcomer, bestowing a sultry smile on him. The new arrival glanced at her, eyes narrowing very slightly.

Then Lissa's attention was diverted. A hand came down on her bare arm.

'I feel like dancing,' one of the two men at her table announced.

Hiding her reluctance, Lissa smiled as if delighted, and got to her feet. Just beyond the bar was a small dance area where the music was coming from. She was grateful it was upbeat and fast, requiring little more than jerky gyration. But two minutes later the music segued into a slow number, and her escort slid his hands around her waist. She tried not to flinch, though she hated close dancing with punters.

Then, abruptly, there was someone else there.

Xavier let the blonde hang on his sleeve, but he took no notice of her. His attention was entirely focussed on his mark.

Lissa Stephens.

In the flesh. And no different from the photo in the dossier. Blonde hair, backcombed and sprayed for volume, far too much make-up, and a figure moulded tightly in a cheap satin dress. For a moment a stab of black rage speared him that such a blatantly tarty female could embroil his idiotic brother. What the hell did Armand see in her?

'I adore dancing,' the hostess at his side gushed breathily.

Xavier could hear her accent—Polish, Russian, something in that region. Presumably she'd come to London in the hope of a better life than she would have at home. He felt a flicker of compunction. For so many of the former Eastern Bloc life was tough, and he couldn't blame such women for trying to improve their economic circumstances, even if in distasteful ways such as being a casino hostess, or worse. Then his eyes hardened again. That allowance might be made for immigrants, but could it extend to someone like Lissa Stephens? She'd grown up with the advantages of a free education, free health care and, if necessary, free housing. So what need was there for her to work in a place like this—unless she chose to? And what did it say about a woman who *wanted* a job like this?

Time to move in on Lissa Stephens and take her measure close up.

He walked to where she was dancing in a clinch.

'My dance,' he said.

The man swivelled his head belligerently. Xavier dealt with him first.

'Trade?' he invited.

The man looked past his shoulder at the blonde Slavic beauty hovering, who clearly outshone his existing dance partner. Instantly his belligerence vanished.

'Deal,' he said, his voice only slightly slurred. He dropped his current partner and pasted a big smile on his face at the woman at Xavier's side, sweeping her off into a dance. Judging by her peeved expression, the girl hadn't wanted the trade—but Xavier couldn't care less. He turned his attention to his target.

In the dim, flashing light she looked no different close up, except for her slight air of being taken aback.

'Shall we?' he said, and not waiting for an answer took her into his arms.

She stiffened like a board.

Surprise flickered in him—it was an out-of-place reaction for her to make. Instinctively, he eased back a little, drawing some distance between them.

'What is it?' he asked.

Something moved in her eyes, then it was gone. A smile stretched her mouth.

'Hi—I'm Lissa,' she said, her voice husky, ignoring his comment.

The smile widened. Or did it strain, rather, as if it were an effort? Xavier dismissed the momentary speculation. His hands

rested on her waist, and through the cheap satin he could feel the curve of her body. His eyes surveyed her face.

There was no hardness in her expression now. Instead there was only blankness. Close up, her make-up was atrocious. Layered on over her skin, cracking already around her nostrils, her eyes caked in shadow and her lashes in thick mascara. And as for her mouth—

Her crimson lipstick was like jam, sticky and thick.

Revulsion shimmered through him. No woman of his acquaintance—and his acquaintance with women was extensive—would ever have done what this girl had done to her face! The women in his world, Madeline and her friends, were all chic, elegant, and their make-up was immaculate. They were from a different species than the woman he was dancing with. Disdain edged his eyes.

Then, catching himself, he concealed it. It would not serve his purpose to let it show. Deliberately making himself relax, he looked down into her face.

'So, Lissa—do you think you'll bring me good luck at the tables?'

He smiled encouragingly. Again, just for a moment, she seemed to stiffen in his arms. Then it was gone.

'I'm sure you'll be lucky,' she said. Once more the smile seemed to stretch right across her mouth.

'Fine by me,' Xavier answered. 'Let's go.'

He dropped his hands from her, and just for a second she seemed to sway slightly. He ignored it, and started to usher her from the dance floor, effortlessly guiding her forward, across the bar area and into the gaming rooms. He could just about feel the manager's eyes on him, greedily eyeing him up. A cynical twist pulled at his mouth. Well, he would oblige the proprietors of this third-rate establishment and lose sufficient money to be sure of a welcome return.

Should one be necessary, of course.

Although he very much doubted it would be. His eyes narrowed, focussing on the over-laquered hair bouncing on Lissa Stephens's bared shoulders, on her derriere, swaying as she walked in front of him on her high heels. Already, his worst assumptions were being confirmed. Lissa Stephens looked to be exactly what he had feared she was—a woman he could never permit his brother to marry.

Lissa all but collapsed on a high-perched chair at the blackjack table. What on earth was going on? Her heart was slugging in her breast, and with her dress as tight as it was that was a bad idea. Her stomach was churning and she was breathless to boot. Desperately she tried to get her head together—and failed completely. All she could do was cling to the chair and try and keep going.

But it was hard—horribly hard.

Two realities had just slammed into each other, and the result was carnage. She could cope with one reality, but not both. The sordid reality of having to work in this place, looking so tarty, having to smile at complete strangers and coax them to buy extortionately priced bad champagne, was only bearable so long as she could mentally dismiss each and every punter that she had to 'be nice' to. She couldn't, absolutely couldn't, let any of them get to her—for any reason whatsoever.

But the man who was now coolly picking up his cards got to her all right—slamming into her with a reality that had a physical impact on her. Got to her in the same way as being run over by a bus got to you. Knocking every breath of air out of your lungs so that all you could do was swallow and gaze helplessly.

Except that gazing was the one thing she knew, with every last shred of effort, she must not do. Yet the urge to do so was overwhelming. His physical presence at her side was overwhelming. When he had walked up to her on the dance floor and disengaged her from her partner, with a single line in a continental accent

that had curled inside her, it had been overwhelming, and when he had slid his hands around her waist and drawn her towards him she had completely frozen. Yet her heart had been thumping like a trip hammer, her whole body as tense as a board with awareness of the man.

As her fingers tightened now on the ornamental arms of the chair she felt a wave of reaction go through her. This was all wrong. Wrong and horrible, and… Well, just wrong and horrible. Because to have a man like that—who just took your breath away—paying attention to you, any attention at all, in a place like this, when you looked like a cheap trashy tart, was just excruciating. She wanted to run, bolt, hide with mortification.

With a sharp, painful inhalation of breath she forced some composure into herself. What the hell had she to be mortified about? OK, so the guy was as out of place here as a diamond on a rhinestone necklace. But he was here, wasn't he? So that meant that, however fancy he was, he was still just a punter. So what the hell did it matter that he was the most incredible-looking male she'd ever set eyes on outside a movie?

And anyway… Another harsh truth hit her squarely in the face. She'd been so preoccupied trying to come to grips with the impact the man had on her that she was only now registering it.

Whatever the reason he'd swapped Tanya for her, it was not because he wanted to eye her up. There had been nothing in his expression to indicate that he found her attractive.

Her mouth tightened momentarily. Good God, how on earth should a man who looked like he did find a woman who looked the way she did right now attractive? Only the sleazeballs here ever made eyes at her—a man like the one beside her now wouldn't look twice at some tarty hostess with bad make-up and worse hair.

Just for a second, a pang went through her.

If he could only see her the way she *could* look…

She slammed the thought shut. The girl she had once been, with the time and the *joie de vivre* to make the most of the looks she had been born with, to find fun in flirtation and dating, didn't exist any more. Hadn't done since the screech of tyres and the sickening shock of metal impacting upon metal had destroyed everything she had so blithely taken for granted till then. Now life had reduced itself to the hard, cruel essentials, to the unrelenting grind to try, so desperately, to achieve the one goal to which she had now dedicated her life.

As for her looks—well, they had got her this job, and she could be glad of that at least. And she could be glad, she knew, that the cheap, tacky, tarty look she had to adopt here was actually a protection for her. Any man who leered or letched over her looking the way she did now would be the very last to appeal to her. Her hostess image was almost like armour against the sleaziness of her job.

A job she had to do, like it or not. So there was no point wishing she could just walk out of the door and never come back. Steeling her spine, she deliberately let her gaze go to the blackjack table, watching the play.

Fast as the cards moved, she could see that the man at her side was not playing the odds, and was therefore losing repeatedly. She frowned inwardly. The guy did not look like a loser. Just the opposite.

She gave a mental shrug. So what if the guy dropped money as if it was litter? What did she care? Her only job was to get him to buy as much champagne as she could and stay the distance until her shift was over, then she could finally get home. And sleep.

'I'm sure some champagne would turn your luck,' she ventured purringly, forcing her voice into a kind of caressing simper. Even as she spoke she felt revulsion shimmer through her. God, this was a sordid job all right. Crass and tacky and vulgar.

Well, tough—the familiar litany bit through her: she needed

money and she just couldn't be too fussy about how she got it, so she must just get on with it and do it.

She stretched her mouth in its usual fake smile, and tilted her head invitingly. From the corner of her eye she saw Jerry, one of the waiters who circulated endlessly with trays of ready-filled champagne glasses.

The man at Lissa's side straightened slightly, and turned to look at her. For just a second she felt she was being bored right through by a laser beam, and then, just as abruptly, it was gone. Now there was only a veiled look in the dark, long-lashed eyes that she could not look into.

He gave the slightest shrug.

'Why not?' he responded, and, glancing past her, beckoned Jerry with a single flick of his index finger, relieving him of two foaming glasses and handing one to Lissa. Carefully she took it, ensuring she did not touch the man's fingers. Even so she felt her stomach tighten yet again.

'So, do you think I should try the roulette table?'

His Gallic-accented voice quivered down her spine, upsetting all the toughly held defences she needed in a place like this. Oh, hell—why, oh, why, was this happening? It was just all wrong—all out of place. A man like this, and her in a place like this, looking the way she did, acting out this distasteful farce. She took a gulp of champagne as if it would help her steel her nerves. Forcing herself, she made herself smile at him.

Don't look at his eyes. Look at him, but don't see him. Look through him. Pretend he's just one of the regular punters. Pretend it's all just normal, perfectly normal.

She could feel her jaw aching with the tension in it as she held her bright, false smile, her gaze, by supreme force of effort, not quite meeting his.

'Oh, good idea!' she exclaimed vacuously. 'I'm sure you'll win at roulette.' She lifted her glass. 'Here's to Lady Luck,' she

toasted brightly, and took another gulp of champagne. She drank as little as she could while she was working, but right now she felt she needed all the help she could find to get through this excruciating ordeal.

As she lowered her glass it registered that he hadn't actually drunk anything at all. Given the quality of the champagne, she was hardly surprised—but then why buy it? For the dozenth time she gave a deliberate mental shrug. Nothing, *nothing* about this man who for some bizarre and inexplicable reason was in this casino, and for some even more bizarre, even more inexplicable reason was keeping her by his side, was of the slightest concern to her. He was a punter—her sole task was to get him to spend money, and that was all.

Carefully, she slid off the high chair, trying not to wince as her tired, sore feet hit the floor.

Roulette proved just as much of an ordeal as blackjack had. Yet again she had to sit beside him, too close, and watch him reach forward, to place his chips on the squares. This time, because roulette was more random—though the odds were always, as ever, stacked in favour of the house—he did win from time to time. But he played carelessly, as if it didn't bother him in the slightest whether he won or lost. Opposite, Lissa could see Tanya making eyes at him—to no avail.

Finally, when the last of his chips were gone, and with a slight shake of his head he'd countered the croupier's offer of more, he turned to Lissa.

'*Tant pis.*' He gave a shrug to dismiss his losses.

She made herself smile.

'Bad luck,' she said. It was inane, but expected.

An eyebrow rose. 'Do you think so? I think we make our own luck in life, *n'est ce pas?*'

Something shadowed in Lissa's eyes. *Did* you make your own luck in life? Or was it external, arbitrary—cruel? Did luck

turn in the blink of an eye, transforming happiness to tragedy in the space of a few moments?

The swerve of wheels, the speed of a car, minute seconds of inattention. And instant, devastating tragedy—destroying in moments the happiness of everyone. Destroying more than happiness…so much more.

Her eyes hardened.

Xavier saw the change in her expression—the hardness in it suddenly. It stirred an answering hardness in him. Lissa Stephens, like the Russian girl, or any of the others here, would be a woman who made her own luck—and it would be at the expense of men.

But not—his expression darkened—at the expense of his vulnerable, good-hearted brother.

His eyes flickered briefly over the girl's face. All his forebodings were proving true—the very thought of Armand entrapped by this excuse for a woman in any way whatsoever was abhorrent. As his own revulsion at the vulgar, tarty image the girl presented impacted in his mind, so, too, did the conviction that his brother could not possibly know what this 'woman of his dreams' did for a living.

Well…Xavier's eyes hardened again momentarily. This was exactly why he'd interrupted his own business schedule—why he'd despatched Armand to visit XeL's key retailers in Dubai, with instructions to fly straight on to New York from the Emirates to do likewise there. So that he would have the opportunity to make a dispassionate, deliberate investigation into what Lissa Stephens was.

And, whilst he was grimly convinced that he now had all the evidence he needed to condemn the girl as fulfilling the worst of his fears, he would, nevertheless, move on to the next stage as he had planned. He shot back his cuff and glanced at his watch.

'*Hélas*, I must go. I have an early morning meeting tomorrow. *Bon soir*, *mademoiselle*—and thank you for your company.'

He bestowed a smile on her, somewhere between perfunctory and courteous, and moved off. Lissa watched him go. Wearily, she brushed her forehead. A tight band was pressing around it. Tiredness swept over her in a wave—tiredness and depression.

What was the point of her responding to a man like that? None at all. Even if she hadn't been working in a place like this, looking like a cheap tart, she still would have had no business registering anything about him. Her life had no room, no time, for anything other than what filled it now.

Guilt shafted through her. Oh, God, how could she dare complain about her lot when she had nothing worth complaining about? Nothing whatsoever compared with—

She shut her mind off. The incredibly disturbing Frenchman had achieved one good thing. He had mopped up the rest of her time here, and now she could go home at last.

A bare ten minutes later, back in normal clothes again, hair vigorously brushed free of backcombing and lacquer, face stripped of its caking make-up, she plunged out into the London night.

CHAPTER THREE

IT WAS chill and raw and spattering with rain, but she didn't care. After the smoke and cheap perfume and the smell of alcohol in the casino, the dirty London air smelt fresh and clean in comparison. She took a lungful, lifting her face into the drizzle, hands plunging deep into her padded jacket pockets. She was wearing jeans and a comfortable jumper, and flat heeled ankle boots good for walking briskly. Her long hair, in need of a wash after all the lacquer, was brushed off her face into a high ponytail that dipped down her back as she lifted her face. Like one released from prison, she strode off along the narrow alleyway the back of the casino opened onto and made for the more brightly lit street beyond, where her bus stop was.

She walked swiftly—not just because looking sure and purposeful was one of her safety precautions at this time of night in this part of London, but also because she was cutting it fine to catch the night bus she needed to take her south of the river at this early hour of the morning. If she missed the bus it would be well over half an hour until the next one.

As she headed briskly towards the bus stop, a hundred metres away on the other side of the road, the rain intensified. The few cars heading along the road threw up water as they passed, but just as she paused at the kerbside to dart across the road to the

stop, impatient to cross because she could see her bus approaching, a large car came right past her, too close to the kerb. Its rear wheels caught a puddle that had formed and water sprayed up at her, soaking into her jeans. She gave a start of annoyance, jumping back instinctively. But what annoyed her even more was that the car, a sleek, black expensive-looking saloon, had promptly stopped dead. It was blocking her path across the road, and she could only, with a mutter of exasperation, dodge around the back of the car, wait for another car to swoosh past, and then hurry across the road. The bus was almost at her stop. She wasn't going to get to the far side in time to flag it down, and unless someone happened to be using that stop—which they never did—it would just sail by.

Which was exactly what it did, just as Lissa had reached the traffic island in the middle of the roadway.

Damn, damn, damn.

She stared, tight-mouthed, after the departing bus. Her shoulders sagged in depression. Over thirty minutes to wait in the cold and wet—and she wouldn't get home for well over an hour now. And she was so tired.

'Mademoiselle?'

Her head swivelled as she turned abruptly. The door of the car that had sprayed her and then blocked her crossing was open, and someone was half leaning out from the rear seat.

It was the Frenchman from the casino.

Even as her stomach gave an automatic, treacherous flip, the rest of her body stiffened.

The car door opened more widely, making a passing car swerve slightly. The Frenchman was getting out, crossing over to her as she stood, marooned, on the traffic island. He was wearing a black cashmere overcoat, superbly tailored, making him look even more of a knockout, and Lissa's stomach gave another flip at the image he made.

'It is…Lissa…is it not? I almost did not recognise you.'

Dark eyes flicked over her, registering the completely different appearance she now had. There was surprise in them. Open surprise. And something more. Something that had not been in them before.

'I hope you will forgive me—were you trying to catch the bus that has just gone?'

'Yes,' answered Lissa tersely. Annoyance and exasperation were still uppermost in her emotions. But another emotion was welling up in her—an emotion she didn't want and pushed back down hard. It had to do with the expression in the cashmere-coated Frenchman's eyes.

'*Je suis désolé*. First my car splashes you—now I have caused you to miss your bus. I hope, therefore, that you will permit me to offer you a lift instead?'

His voice was smooth. Far too smooth beneath the regret he professed to be feeling at what he had done to her.

Her eyes flashed.

'Thank you, no. There will be another bus shortly. Excuse me.' She turned her back and strode across the remainder of the road to the bus stop. The rain had got heavier, and the bus stop had no shelter. She hunched her shoulders and tried not to shiver. The wet material of her jeans felt cold on her shins. She did not look at the Frenchman.

At the traffic island, Xavier looked after her for a moment. Her reaction had surprised him. But right now surprise was too mild a word for what he was experiencing. Shock would be more appropriate.

And understanding. Belated, but like a punch through his system.

At last it made sense why Armand was bewitched by this girl.

Stripped of the casino hostess outfit and the gross make-up and hairdo, the girl was quite simply a knockout, even making no attempt whatsoever to look good. He could see at a glance

what the layers of overdone, tarty make-up had so successfully concealed. She had a beauty to catch and hold every male eye.

Emotions twisted inside him. Contradictory, powerful—unwelcome.

He pushed the emotions aside. They were unnecessary, and getting in his way. He must not pay them attention—all his focus now must be on the next stage of his agenda for dealing with Armand's bombshell. The incident just now had been carefully timed and executed, with one of his security men reporting exactly when Lissa Stephens had left the casino, to allow his driver the precise amount of time to make the manoeuvre he just had.

He crossed back to the car and climbed in.

'Circle to the bus stop,' he instructed.

He folded himself into the deep interior, bracing himself slightly as the car moved forward in a tight turn to draw up again on the other side of the street. Once more he opened the door, this time to the pavement. To his satisfaction, the rain was now falling steadily in heavy rods. She would be soaking wet in minutes if she didn't get in the car.

He leaned forward, holding the car door open invitingly.

'Please accept my offer of a lift, *mademoiselle*—this is not the weather to do otherwise.' He made it sound as though she were being childish in her refusal.

A stony glare was cast in his direction for his pains.

'I'm afraid I don't get into cars with complete strangers,' Lissa answered shortly.

Wordlessly, Xavier slid his hand into his inside jacket pocket and extracted a business card. It was a calculated gamble. Armand had told him he had said nothing to his intended bride of his connection with XeL. Now would be the moment when he would find out whether that was indeed true—and whether the ambitious Mademoiselle Stephens had been doing any checking of her own into just how rich a fish she had caught. Would

the card, with its simple 'Xavier Lauran—XeL', without any title or position added, register with her?

Covertly, he studied her reaction as, reluctantly, she took the card and studied it in the orange glare of the streetlight.

All her face revealed was a slight frown.

'XeL—is that the posh luggage company?' she asked, as she lifted her eyes from the card.

Xavier felt a flare of annoyance at the casual description.

'Among other items,' he replied, in the same dry voice. '*Mademoiselle*, I do not wish to appear impatient, but do you intend to accept my offer of a lift or not?'

For a moment, he could tell—and the knowledge sent another flare of annoyance through him—she hung in the balance. Then, abruptly, she spoke.

'Oh, all right, then. I might as well.' It was hardly a gracious acceptance, and once again Xavier felt a flare of annoyance go through him. She started forward, and Xavier moved to the other side of the back seat. She settled herself into the vacated space and yanked at the seat belt, turning to him as the car started to pull out into the road.

'If it's not too much out of your way, could you let me out at Trafalgar Square? There are more night buses from there.' She spoke sharply still—the result of frustration at having missed her bus, annoyance with herself for succumbing to the temptation of the lift, and of a reason she had absolutely no intention of acknowledging. Not sitting this close to him. Her sharpness was a defence she needed right now.

Xavier lifted an eyebrow. 'You do not wish to be driven home all the way?'

'I live south of the river,' she answered, in the same short tone. 'It's miles out of your way.'

'*C'est ne fait rien.*' He spoke with indifference. 'It is of no consequence.'

She looked at him. Her expression was acidly sceptical. 'You said in the casino you had an early meeting—you will hardly want to go careering across London at this hour of the night.'

Xavier cast her a caustic look again. 'I said that merely because I wanted to leave—and I did not want any persuasions to change my mind.'

Was there a flash in her eye? He could not tell in the dim light. What he could tell, though—and he was still coming to terms with the knowledge—was that she had a bone structure that was still impacting on him. And that he did not need, for reasons that he did not want to think about at this moment, when his sole focus must be on the task in hand.

But even though he was trying to suppress it, to his intense annoyance he realised that a seismic shift was taking place inside his head. Some mental fault line was realigning—realigning in a way that made him want to do nothing more right now except study in detail the extraordinary metamorphosis performed on the woman in front of him. How could he possibly have known how different she would look without the gross make-up and the hostess outfit? The question was rhetorical, and he knew it—but knowing it made no difference. He still felt as if he'd been hit on the head with a blunt object.

Urgently he fought back—fought back not just against the seismic shockwave that had crunched through him, but against what it brought in its wake. He knew the name of what that was, but he would not, could not acknowledge what it was. Could not admit it even to himself.

It doesn't matter. This transformation alters nothing. All it does was explain how she's managed to fool Armand. He'd obviously only seen the image she was currently presenting—not the image of the evening.

Because, he reasoned harshly, slamming down that iron control even more tightly over his reactions, it was the *putain*

version of Lissa Stephens that was the one he had to remember—
the one that was endangering his brother, the one that made her
completely unsuitable to marry him. So what if she suddenly, out
of nowhere, had turned everything he'd taken her for on its head?
It changed nothing.

But even as he forced the words into his mind he knew them
for a lie. Knew that the shock to his system was still ricocheting
through him even as he fought to catch and control it.

'If your driver goes down Piccadilly, he can cut through to
Trafalgar Square.'

The girl's voice cut through Xavier's thoughts.

'It is no problem to drive you to your home,' he answered.

Again, as he spoke, Lissa's back went up almost automatically. 'Nevertheless,' she said stonily, 'I would prefer to be let
out in Trafalgar Square.'

She eyed him suspiciously. She was already regretting her im-
pulsive action in climbing into the car. OK, so he'd shown her a
business card—but so what? Xavier Lauran of XeL might be
some fancy French businessman, in a league that was light years
from the kind of businessmen that frequented the casino, but he
was still just another punter for all that. No way was she prepared
to let him drive her home. It wasn't even a public taxi—God
knew what he and his driver might have planned for her. Unease
prickled over her skin.

For a moment, in the uncertain light of the streets, she
thought she saw a momentary expression in the man's eyes.
Then it was gone.

He gave a slight shrug. It seemed a very Gallic gesture.

'*Comme tu veux—*'

'Yes, I do wish—thank you.' Again, her voice was clipped.

For a moment the dark eyes rested on her. Their expression
was unreadable.

He was too close. Too close in this car—too…

Intimate. That was the word. In the confines of the car he seemed far closer than he had in the casino. That was because in the casino, even though she might be crushed up next to a punter at a table, or perched beside him at the gaming table, or even dancing with him, the place was so public. The ambience was so off-putting that she never felt any real physical proximity.

But this...

Automatically she coiled back into her corner of the seat. It made no difference. He was still far, far too close.

And he was looking at her.

Worse than looking. He was seeing her. Seeing her as she really was. The real person, not the facsimile of a cheap hostess she had to be at the casino.

If only she still had her make-up on. She might look like a tart with it, but it served as a mask, a protective mask. Hiding her, the real her, from the punters and the other girls at the casino.

Hiding her from this man who had made her stomach flip full circle in the first moment of registering his appearance.

But she couldn't hide from him now. Now, in the shadowy confines of this car he'd picked her up in, she was completely, absolutely exposed to him. An invisible shiver went through her—trepidation, alarm, and something quite, quite different. For a moment longer she went on looking at him, feeling her eyes widen, her focus start to blur. Dear God, he was just *so* incredible to look at...

'Tu parles Français?' His voice had sharpened.

'Oui, un peu. Pourquoi?' retorted Lissa, taken aback by the sudden question. And all too aware, with the same disturbing mix of resentment and that other reaction she would not acknowledge, that he had used the *tu* form of address—the one reserved, when it came to adults, to indicate either superiority or intimacy.

His response told her exactly which form he had intended—and it was like a cold shower of water. 'Because foreign language

skills are unusual in girls like you. Unless they are foreign to begin with,' came the blunt answer.

Lissa felt a spike of antagonism go through her. 'Oh,' she said. 'Girls like me? I see.' Her voice was flat. 'You mean girls too thick to do anything other than work as a hostess?'

'Thick?' There was a slight frown between his eyes.

'*Bête,*' Lissa supplied helpfully, with a tight, humourless smile. Resentment curdled in her. Oh, Xavier Lauran might be God's gift to the discerning woman, but he was as full of prejudice as any other male when it came to the assumptions he made.

'*Enfin*, if you are clever enough to speak a language foreign to you, why do you do the work you do?' The cool challenge of his voice made Lissa's chin lift. There was something else in his voice as he spoke, but she was too resentful to identify it.

'I might as well ask why a man of your evident intelligence and background chooses to patronise the kind of place I work in?' she countered sharply.

His face shuttered. Oh, she thought nastily, he doesn't like it when some tarty little casino hostess dares to question his behaviour.

'Why do you work there?'

The question shot at her. Quite ignoring the one she'd just thrown at him.

'It's a job,' she answered flatly.

She looked away. It was an instinctive gesture. She didn't want to see the expression in the man's eyes. She knew it would be condemning. And that in itself would worsen the curdling mix of resentment and self-revulsion she always felt whenever she had to face up to how she earned money.

I don't have any choice! She wanted to yell at him. But what was the point? A familiar wave of weariness and depression washed over her. Then, as it passed through her, she became aware that the car was already at Trafalgar Square, and was

turning to go under Admiralty Arch and down the Mall towards Buckingham Palace.

'You've gone too far,' she exclaimed, her head twisting round to the Frenchman again before she leaned forward to get the attention of the driver.

'I said I would take you home,' came the reply, and yet again Lissa got the feeling the man was not used to being questioned.

'No.'

Her voice was flat. Adamant.

Xavier looked at her. Curious, he registered. There was something more than negation in that voice. Something that was more akin to…

Fear. That was what it was. His pupils pinpricked as they rested on her face.

Yes, that was what was flaring in her eyes right now. There was not doubt of it. And more than fear, too. He had seen it momentarily in the casino, and he had seen it again just now, when she'd turned her face from him. It *jagged* an emotion in him— one that had absolutely no place in the situation. But it was there all the same.

What he had seen in her face was there again now, taut behind the fear flaring in her eyes.

Tiredness.

Quite evident, quite unmistakeable, exposed in the gaunt contours around her eyes. The girl looked exhausted.

'*Mademoiselle,* it is no trouble to conduct you to your flat. There is little traffic at this hour, and the detour will not be significant. It is because of me that you missed your bus—permit me to make amends.'

Lissa sat back, looking at him. His voice was different. She couldn't tell why, but it was all the same. It was kinder. For some strange, unaccountable reason she felt her throat tighten. She didn't want this man being kind to her. He was just a

stranger. A man who frequented the casino she had to work in because she had no choice—a man who was, therefore, nothing more than a punter. She didn't want him being kind to her, doing her favours.

'It really isn't necessary,' she began stiffly. 'I couldn't impose on you.'

He silenced her objection. 'It is no imposition,' he returned, and now the kindness was gone. There was only an impersonal indifference. 'I need to make several phone calls now to the USA. Whether I make them from my hotel or from this car is irrelevant.'

As if to prove his point, he slid a long-fingered hand inside his luxurious overcoat and withdrew a mobile phone, flicking it open with an elegant twist of his wrist.

'Give my driver your address,' he instructed. Then he started up the phone and proceeded to punch a stored number.

For a moment Lissa just went on looking at him uncertainly. Outside, the tall trees lining the Mall flashed past with the expensively smooth ride the flash car afforded, and then they were circling around the Queen Victoria monument, wheeling past the illuminated Victorian baroque splendour of Buckingham Palace.

Xavier Lauran lifted the phone to his ear and started to talk. His French was far too rapid for Lissa even to attempt to follow it. He was clearly absorbed in the conversation. For a moment she allowed herself the pleasure of listening to his beautifully timbred voice, fluent in its own language.

Then the chauffeur was twisting his head briefly.

'If you give me your address, *Mademoiselle?*' His accent was French, too, but it did not shiver down her nerves like that of his employer.

Lissa gave in. Surely she was safe enough? Would a man who was evidently some kind of senior executive in a prestigious international company really risk any kind of scandal?

Resignedly, she gave her address, and then sat back. As the car headed down Victoria Street towards Parliament Square and the River Thames, she leaned back farther in her seat. The leather seats were deep and soft. Across from her the devastating Frenchman was paying her no more attention than if she was a block of wood, his mellifluous voice rising and falling rapidly, letting her catch nothing more than the briefest word every now and then. Outside, the flickering lights of an almost deserted London strobed in her vision. She closed her eyes to shut it out. Weariness swept down over her. She was so tired she could sleep for a thousand years and not wake.

The warmth of the car stole through her. Her breathing slowed. She slept.

In the opposite corner of the passenger seat, Xavier paused in his interrogation of his west coast sales director. His eyes rested on her.

His thoughts were mixed. Contradictory.

The sharp shadows of her face in the streetlight set her cheekbones into relief. Long lashes swept down over her pale cheeks. In repose, her tiredness seemed to have ebbed, leaving nothing behind except the question as to why Lissa Stephens should look so tired when she had all day to sleep.

And another question, as well. Far more troubling.

Why did he feel a stab of pity at her being so tired—and why did the exhaustion in her face merely emphasise the extraordinary beauty of her bone structure?

He wanted to go on looking at her—just looking.

Then his sales director was telling him the next set of figures. With a mixture of reluctance and relief Xavier resumed his conversation. Deliberately he looked away from the girl.

Inside him, the same confused flux of emotions continued to recycle.

Emotions that were completely, absolutely, out of place

when all that was required was the cool, analytical application of reason.

Yet they continued to circle all the same—to his irritation and displeasure.

'I believe we have arrived.'

The words, murmured without expression, stirred Lissa to wakefulness. She felt dopey, her mind blurred and unable to focus. Then, with a little shake, she roused herself fully from the torpid slumber the warmth and motion of the car had induced in her.

She sat upright with an effort. The car had paused by the kerb just outside a rundown Victorian apartment block, built in the nineteenth century as social housing for the labouring poor. Unlike many parts of South London, this area had not gentrified, but the virtue of that was that it made the rent of the one-bedroom flat affordable to her. The last thing she needed was to squander money on accommodation.

She blinked. 'Thank you. It was really very kind of you.'

Her voice was slightly husky with sleep, but she made herself look at the man who'd insisted on driving her home. As her eyes lifted to his face, she felt the same catch in her breath she'd had when she'd first set eyes on him. Weakness flushed through her, and a sense of disbelief that she was really here, sitting in the same car as him. For a self-indulgent moment she just went on looking at him. His face was slightly averted from her, glancing out of his window at the locality. Did his expression tighten? She didn't know—only knew that the shadows of the car's interior only served to accentuate the incredible contours of his face.

Then his head turned fully towards her, and his eyes came to meet hers.

Her stomach hollowed. In her still-dopey state she could not

tear her own gaze away. She felt her eyes cling to his, in a moment of exchange that was like a bolt through her.

Then, *'Mademoiselle?'*

The cold draught of air at her side and the polite voice of the driver made her realise that the passenger door had been opened. They were waiting for her to get out, the chauffeur and the flash Frenchman.

She broke eye contact and got out.

'Thank you for the lift. It was very kind of you,' she repeated, her voice stilted. As she got out her key, she allowed herself one more glance back at the car. It hovered by the side of the road, sleek and dark and expensive. Like the man inside.

She could not see him now—he was just a darker shadow in the dark interior. Something pierced inside her. That was it, then. The last time she'd see him. That moment before she'd got out of the car. Already the driver was climbing back into his seat, closing his own door. Jerkily, she turned away, and opened the door and went inside.

Behind her, she heard the car glide away into the night.

Xavier stared unseeingly ahead of him. The street was scruffy and rundown, with litter blowing around and the dank, bleak dreariness of poverty. Not a good place to live. No wonder Lissa Stephens was eager for a way out of here.

His eyes darkened. But *not* at the expense of his brother.

He waited for the stab of anger to come—but instead all that came was a repeat of that sense of jarring disconcertion he'd felt when he'd set eyes on her by the bus stop and almost failed to recognise her as the same woman he'd deliberately singled out for his attention in the casino.

How could she look so different? The question sliced through him again, and once more he could give no rational explanation for the difference it made to him. It shouldn't make a difference.

Yet it did.

And another thought was intruding—where it had no business to be.

If she looked that good without even trying, what would she look like if she were properly dressed and presented?

Immediately, without volition, his mind was there. That long blonde hair, loose but sleek, flicked back off her face, make-up subtle but enhancing the natural beauty she possessed, and her slender body gowned as a beautiful woman should always be gowned.

The image hovered in his mind. Vivid. Powerful. Alluring.

No. He would *not* sit here fantasising about what Lissa Stephens might look like if she were done up the way she would be if he were inviting her to spend the evening with him.

More than the evening.

No. Again he slammed the harsh, forbidding negative down across his wayward thoughts. The only reason he had anything at all to do with Lissa Stephens was to assess whether she was suitable to marry his brother. It had seemed in the casino an open and shut case. Picking her up in the street as he'd done should only have confirmed it. She should have been eager to be picked up—eager for the interest and intention of someone so obviously rich. She should have batted her thickened eyelashes at him and come on to him.

Instead, she'd shown every reluctance at getting into his car, and when she had she'd fallen asleep.

He frowned. It didn't make sense. It was irrational. Lissa Stephens in the casino and Lissa Stephens asleep in his car seemed two quite different people, both in appearance and in behaviour.

As the car drove on, back into the brightly lit affluent West End, a world away from the dreary bleakness of south London's poorer districts, Xavier knew he could be sure only of one thing. That he could not yet be sure about Lissa Stephens.

His investigation, he had to accept, was very far from over.

But what, precisely, should be his next step?

Well… He shifted his shoulders as if to release a sudden tension. He had the rest of the night to decide.

The rest of the night to think about Lissa Stephens.

As she stood outside the door to her ground-floor flat, Lissa paused a moment. Her emotions were strange. She was still feeling blurred from interrupted sleep. But that was not the reason.

The reason was even now driving away down the street.

Why did he do it? Why did he offer me a lift and go out of his way to drive me back here, miles away?

Any wariness that he might have had less than honourable intentions had been completely unfounded. He hadn't made the slightest attempt to make a move on her, and certainly her own attitude had scarcely been inviting.

Deliberately so. Because what, dear God, would have been the point? Even without any of the complications in her life, the guy was still a punter, and therefore completely out of bounds. He might be like something out of Continental movie in terms of looks, but if he'd actually thought he might pick her up sexually, knowing her to be a casino hostess, it would only have been because he himself was a sleazeball.

But he wasn't that.

Apart from that moment when he'd shown surprise that a woman working as a hostess could possibly be capable of learning a foreign language, he hadn't actually dissed her at all. In fact, if she'd had to describe his attitude towards her she would have had to say it was one of civility and nothing more.

She frowned again. So why had he offered her a lift? Some kind of Gallic gallantry after making her miss her bus? If so, it had been an over-the-top gesture, and she'd responded appropriately by asking to be let out at Trafalgar Square. He could have done that and gone on his way.

But he hadn't. He'd insisted on driving her all the way back here. But why?

Impatiently she brushed the question from her head. It was pointless asking it—she wasn't going to get an answer. And the answer didn't matter anyway.

Xavier Lauran was not someone she was going to encounter a second time after all.

For the briefest moment, as she inserted her key into the lock and turned it quietly, she felt a pang go through her. He had walked into her life—and out again. The most incredible-looking male she'd ever seen. A man to take her breath away, stop the blood in her pulse, hollow out her stomach.

Gone.

The pang bit again. Her eyes clouded. Then, with a tightening of her chin, she let herself inside her flat. Xavier Lauran had been and gone in her life, and that was that. And it was just as well.

There was no room in her life for him. None at all.

No room for anyone except—

'Lissy, you're home.' The voice that spoke out of the darkness was soft, and very slightly slurred.

Lissa walked into the bedroom. Her life closed around her. Familiar, loving, but cruel and bleak.

Xavier stood by the uncurtained windows of his hotel suite and moodily nursed a cognac glass between his fingers. He looked down at the silent street below.

He should go to bed. Go to sleep. But he didn't feel tired. There was a restlessness pacing in his veins. A question circulating in his head.

What was he going to do about Lissa Stephens?

He'd thought it would be cut and dried. That the trashy casino hostess gushing over him was all the evidence he needed that she was the last person he should allow his brother to marry. The

carefully orchestrated offer of a lift was merely supposed to have given the girl the opportunity to do what any of her co-workers would surely have done.

But she hadn't.

Why not?

The cynical answer was that a woman with sufficient—if un-expected—intelligence to have learnt a foreign language was also one that was too smart to jeopardise what she had going with another wealthy man—his brother—to risk a fleeting interlude with anyone else. And maybe that was the reason she hadn't given him the come on.

But maybe it was for a quite different reason. Logic demanded that he consider that possibility. One that was at odds with the woman he had thought she obviously was. Maybe Lissa Stephens simply wasn't the kind of girl the evidence said she was.

The slow, unconscious swirling of the cognac in his glass halted abruptly.

He had to know for sure.

And there was, Xavier knew, with a sudden clenching of his stomach, an obvious way to find out.

Spend more time with her.

Conflicting emotions flashed through him as he articulated the thought—and neither was welcome. Emotion seldom was. But he had to recognise it, all the same. One was extreme reluc-tance—reluctance for a reason that was troublingly evident in the second emotion flaring in him. An emotion that was completely and absolutely inappropriate to the situation. But it was there, all the same—and he could do nothing about it.

Anticipation.

With a sudden lift of his hand, he raised the cognac glass to his lips and took a mouthful of the fine, fiery liquid. He might as well face it—he wanted to see the girl again. Wanted to spend more time with her.

And it was not just to check her out for his brother.

The kick of the cognac to his system seemed to release something in him. A hot pulse through his veins.

He wanted to see her again all right.

Danger prickled on his skin.

He shouldn't do this.

The cool, analytical voice of reason spoke inside his head. It was the voice he always listened to. The voice he ran XeL with, ran his life with—the voice he listened to which had advised him to disentangle his brother from his previous *mésalliance*. It was the voice with which he selected the women for his bed. Suitable women, appropriate women, who moved in his world, who were part of it, and knew the rules by which he conducted his affairs. Women quite unlike the likes of Lissa Stephens, with her confusing double image—one moment a cheap casino hostess and the next...

He shouldn't have thought of Lissa Stephens. Shouldn't have remembered that second image of hers, the one that had come like a blow out of nowhere in a rain-wet London street in the bleak fag end of the night.

But it was too late. It was in his head, etched like a diamond against murky smoke. The pure, bare, unadorned beauty of her profile turned away from him. The long fall of pale hair from its high plume. The upturned collar of her cheap jacket that nevertheless framed the crystal contours of her face.

Of its own volition his hand lifted the glass to his mouth again, and he took another mouthful. He wanted to see that image again. Wanted to look at it. At her.

He needed to know.

The words formed in his mind.

He needed to know. Was she, against all evidence, a fit woman to marry his brother? That was what he needed to find out.

Nothing else. That was, after all, the only question on the table. The only question that could be on the table.

Sharply, he turned away. There was nothing else he needed to know about Lissa Stephens.

As he deposited, with a jerkier movement than was necessary, the cognac glass on a table as he passed it, by heading to his bedroom, he screened out the word that had formed in his consciousness.

Menteur.

Liar.

Lissa lay, staring at the ceiling unseen above her. From time to time, through the muffling of the bedroom door, she could hear a train rattling along the tracks that ran past the rear of the poky flat. From beside her, on the next pillow in the double bed, came the rhythmic rise and fall of slightly stertorous, drug-induced breathing.

She gazed upward into the dark.

For all her extreme weariness she could not sleep. Even though she knew she had to be up again in a few hours, her mind was wide awake.

Thinking. Remembering.

And—worse still—imagining.

About one single face. One single man.

Angrily, she tried to force the image from her mind.

What was the point in thinking about him? None—none at all. So why was she doing it?

Because her mind would not go anywhere else.

Would not even think about the one thing that, above all else in her life, she always thought about. The one person she always had to think about.

Guilt drenched through her. Oh, God—how low could she stoop? Even thinking it with a note of resentment, however faint. Automatically, as if to assuage her own guilt, she reached out a hand to let it rest lightly on the sleeping form beside her. A wave of love and pity welled in her.

If only she could wave a magic wand. If only she could make it somehow instantly better. If only she could…

But she couldn't. Bleakness chilled in her throat. There was no magic wand. Nothing like that. Only a tiny sliver of hope. And even to seize that meant that all her waking hours had to be dedicated to one thing and one thing only—earning money. Saving money. Little by little. Slowly, oh, so slowly.

Unless Armand…

The chill intensified.

He hadn't phoned. She had hoped against hope that tonight he would, but there had been nothing. That made it three nights in a row, not hearing from him.

He's gone.

The grim words tolled in her brain. She might try to dispel them, but they would not disappear.

Gone.

A single word, extinguishing hope—hope she should not have allowed herself.

Against her will the image formed in her mind of sable hair and dark eyes and a sculpted mouth.

CHAPTER FOUR

'LISSA, the manager wants you. In his office. Sharpish!'

Lissa swivelled her head from her cramped place at the vanity unit in the crowded dressing room that she and the other hostesses changed in. She had only just arrived, and was about to start on her make-up.

She frowned at the command, issued by one of the staff from the door.

'What for?'

A shrug was her only answer, and with a sigh Lissa got to her feet again and made her way out of the dressing room. A couple of the other girls looked at her curiously.

The manager's office overlooked the casino floor, which was currently thinly populated.

'You wanted to see me?' said Lissa. She was wary and tense. It was seldom good news when the manager wanted to see a hostess. It was usually to reprimand her for not having brought enough custom to the bar. Maybe, thought Lissa tightly, the manager thought she hadn't got the rich Frenchman to buy enough last night.

Damn, she didn't want to be reminded of him. She'd done her best all day, all through the long slog into the City, and the long, tedious hours working in the office her temping agency had cur-

rently assigned her to. All through the crowded rush-hour journey home, sardined in the Tube train with all the other commuters until they'd been disgorged at the South London underground station closest to her flat. And certainly all through the brief time she'd had at home before setting out for her evening's work here at the casino.

The manager, short and rotund and far from pleasant, eyed her up. Lissa stood impassively.

'Private hire,' he told her. 'You're to go straight there. There's a car waiting outside.'

Lissa stood very still.

'I'm afraid I don't do private hires,' she said quietly. 'I did make that clear when I started.'

The manager narrowed his small eyes.

'You're lucky I'm in a good mood. And *you're* lucky you made a hit last night. The guy who's booked you is that fancy Frog who dropped a ton at the tables. He's paying premium price for you, so make sure you give value for money, all right?'

Lissa swallowed. So Xavier Lauran had not been the type to stoop to coming on to her last night after offering her a lift home? No, he was just the type who liked the euphemism of a 'private hire.'

'Maybe Tanya would—' she ventured.

'He's booked *you*, all right? And you deliver—understand? Or you walk—permanently.'

Lissa understood. Schooling her face into immobility, she nodded and got out. She felt sickened, more than sickened. It just wasn't something she'd thought of the man last night.

Somehow she got herself back downstairs again, picked up her things and left the casino.

Just as last night, the rain was coming down heavily. She shivered, but not because of the wet. She had just lost her job. She knew it. Knew the manager would sack her instantly as soon as he found out she had no intention whatsoever of accepting a

'private hire.' Worse, she wouldn't even get the wages she was owed for this week's work.

Anger and intense depression mingled venomously inside her. Avoiding the front of the casino, she made her way with rapid, urgent footsteps to the main road. At least there were plenty of buses at this time of night, and the Tube was still running. Another thought struck her. What reason could she give for getting home so early? She didn't want to say she'd lost her job because she'd been offered one she wouldn't take.

Well, she would think up something on the way home. She would have to. That was the least of her problems.

Acid still curdled in her stomach, and more than acid. Anger, gall and bitterness. More even than that. But she would not give it words. Instead she found other words.

Creep. Jerk. Slimeball.

She said them in her head, over and over again, pounding them down on the pavement with each hurrying step.

A car pulled on to the pavement ahead of her.

She recognised it instantly. Equally instantly she swerved out on to the roadway in automatic avoidance.

'What are you doing?'

The voice was a demand, wanting an answer. She didn't even look around.

He strode up to her, catching her arm as she tried to plunge through the traffic.

'You'll kill yourself!'

She tried to tear herself free, but he was strong, the grip around her forearm unyielding.

'Let go of me, you total creep.' She tugged again, just as ineffectually. Rain was streaming into her eyes.

'Comment?' The surprise in his voice snapped something in her. She wheeled on him.

'I said let go of me, you creep! You pig! How dare you try

and buy me like that? My God, I might work in that fleapit, but the only work I do is to get jerks like you to buy rip-off drinks. You've got no right to think I do anything else. So take your bloody "private hire" and—'

He said something in French. Abrupt. Basic. Very basic.

His grip tightened on her arm as she stood struggling at the kerbside behind his chauffeured car.

'I do not know what you have been told, but clearly you have been misinformed.'

His voice was icy. Formal. Lissa glared round at him, anger still boiling in her—and still that unwanted awareness of him.

It was a mistake to look at him. Even as she did so she felt again the incredible blow that went right through her solar plexus. The streetlight etched the planes of his face, and the sudden hardness in them, in his eyes, sent an unwilling thrill of reaction through her.

She fought against it.

'Oh, do me a favour,' she threw at him scornfully. 'I wasn't born yesterday. When I get told that you've paid "premium price"—' she emphasised that heavily '—for a "private hire"—' she emphasised that even more heavily '—I don't damn well need it spelt out in neon lights. Nor do I need the creep running the casino to spell it out for me that I either do it or get fired.'

The icy expression in his eyes changed suddenly. Devastatingly. Lissa felt her insides dissolve.

The grip on her arm loosened, but he did not relinquish her. Instead, he guided her up onto the safety of the pavement again.

'Don't—' She hustled back at him, but he ignored her. Then he turned her to face him.

'You take insult,' he informed her, 'where none is intended. At least not by me.' He took a sharp breath. Something changed in his eyes as he looked down at her. Then they were veiled. He dropped her arm. She should have bolted, but she didn't. She just

stood there, in the pelting rain, blinking at him. She didn't know why, but she did all the same.

'I wanted to see you again,' said Xavier Lauran.

Her face didn't change, but something else did, deep inside. She went on blinking at him. Staring at him.

'I wanted to see you again,' he repeated—as if, she thought, he was confirming it to himself.

'Why?' Her question was blunt. Unforgiving.

There was a slight alteration in his features, a lift of his eyebrow.

'Why? Because…' he paused. 'Because when I gave you a lift home yesterday night I…' He fell silent a moment. Then he spoke again. 'You were different,' he said bluntly. 'A quite different woman from the one you had been at the casino. A woman I wanted to see again.'

'What for?' she demanded witheringly. 'Some "private hire" entertainment?'

'For dinner,' he answered simply.

Lissa blinked.

'I wanted to invite you for dinner,' said Xavier Lauran. 'I knew you worked, and I did not know when your night off was. I have limited time in London, so I did not want to waste it. I phoned the casino and asked if it was possible to arrange, as you term it, a "private hire." By that I meant that I would pay the casino for your time, so they would not lose out, and it would free you to accept my invitation to dinner.'

Emotions were churning through her.

'Dinner.' Her voice was flat.

'Just dinner.' His voice was flatter.

She stared up at him. Rain washing down her face.

'Why?' she asked bluntly.

Again, something changed in his eyes, but she didn't know what—not in this uncertain light, with the rain streaming down on both of them. A smile crooked at his mouth. Not much of a

smile, but a smile all the same. A touch sardonic. A touch wry. A touch humorous. A touch indulgent.

'Don't you ever look in the mirror, Lissa? Not in the casino, but at home. When you haven't got all that mess on your face. If you did, you'd have your answer. The reason I want to see you again. The reason I'm inviting you for dinner.'

'Dinner,' she said again. The mouth quirked more.

'I'm a Frenchman,' he elaborated, with that same wry, sardonic touch. 'Dinner is important to me. Tonight I'd like you to share it with me. *Just* dinner,' he added. 'Does that reassure you?' An eyebrow lifted, as if indulging her.

Reassure her? It stunned her. There wasn't another word for it. No word, either, for the hollowing in her stomach as she stood there, frozen, motionless, staring up at Xavier Lauran who had *not,* after all, thought she was a—

'So, will you accept my invitation? Now that you know what it is. And what—' his voice bit suddenly '—it is not.'

'You really mean just dinner?' She could not hide the doubt, the suspicion.

He nodded gravely. 'And, although I do not wish in any way to harass or hurry you, it would, *peut-être*, be considerably appreciated if you would give an imminent answer. On account, you understand—' his eyes glinted '—of the inclement English weather we are currently experiencing.'

She stared at him still. His sable hair was completely wet. So were the shoulders of his cashmere coat. Rain glistened on his eyelashes. They were ridiculously long, she thought abstractedly. Far too long for a man. They ought to make him look feminine, but… Her stomach gave one of the flips it did whenever she stopped blocking out all thoughts of this man who had nothing to do with her life. But feminine was the very last thing they made him look. They simply made him look…

Sexy.

That awful, cheap word. Overused, trashy, tabloid.

And true.

Completely, undeniably true.

She felt her stomach dissolve, gazing up at him, at the way the rain made his hair glisten like a raven's wing, the way it perfected the incredible planes of his face. she just wanted to go on gazing, and gazing and gazing.

He was guiding her towards the car. She hardly registered it. Then the chauffeur was there, opening the passenger door, and she was being ushered inside. She sank back, boneless, into the deep leather seat.

What am I doing?

The question sounded in her mind, but she didn't pay it any attention. She couldn't. She just sat there, capable only of feeling that suddenly she was out of the rain, still soaking wet, but at least not with rain shafting down into her face. A moment later Xavier Lauran had climbed in on his side of the car, and the chauffeur was reclaiming his driving seat.

'Seat belt,' he reminded her, as the car moved off, and his voice, in the confines of the car, suddenly sounded very French.

Very sexy.

No, she mustn't think that word. Not now—not with this man who had walked back into her life when she had thought he never would, never could. And whom up till two minutes ago she had had every reason to think a total jerk, a creep, a slimeball, a—

Punter.

Numbly her eyes flew to him as she fumblingly did up her seat belt. He was currently pulling down his own seat belt with an assured, fluid movement. She wanted to watch him. Wanted to watch him doing anything, everything. Because…

Because she couldn't take her eyes off him. Because he made her stomach go hollow. Because he stopped the breath in her lungs. Because—

He's a punter.

The thought pulled her up short. One of those men who thought spending an evening in a two-bit casino being fawned over by women, drinking third-rate champagne and throwing money around pointlessly on stupid gambling was a good time.

She couldn't do this. Couldn't be here. It was wrong—all wrong.

'What is it?' He'd paused in the act of fastening the seat belt. His eyes focussed on her intently. Questioningly.

'Why did you come to the casino last night?'

Her question was stark.

For a moment he stilled. Then he answered.

'Why do you ask?'

She brushed some raindrops from her hair.

'It's hardly your kind of place, is it?'

He didn't bother to disagree.

'I was bored. I was passing. I'd been to a play in Shaftesbury Avenue I hadn't liked, so I walked out. I didn't feel like going back to my hotel. The casino was an impulse, nothing more, just to pass some time.' His voice was offhand. Then it changed. So did the expression in his eyes.

'But I'm glad I did go in. Because otherwise I wouldn't have met you. And I will tell you, in complete honesty—' he levelled his gaze at her '—that until I saw you at the bus stop last night your appeal to me was precisely zero. But then…' He paused. 'It was unexpected,' he said.

His eyes swept down over her, washing away her guard. She shouldn't let it be washed away, but it was gone all the same.

'It made me want to see you again.'

Simple words.

Doing very unsimple things to her.

He was still looking at her, with that same disarming expression. 'Would it be so very hard to have dinner with me?' he said. There was a quizzical, amused cast to his eye.

Her eyes were uncertain, confused.

She shouldn't do this. She should make him stop the car, get out, go home. Back to her real world. She shouldn't let herself be taken away like this, by a man who did things to her insides that made it impossible to think straight, to think logically, rationally, coolly, sensibly, sanely.

The litany trotted through her head, every word a compelling, urgent argument to tell him to stop the car and let her out. Then into the litany another thought arose, inserting itself into her mind.

If she didn't get out it would mean she'd keep her job at the casino. They wouldn't know she'd just gone for dinner.

But did he really mean just dinner? Was she an idiot to believe him?

'Dinner? That's all?' Her voice was sharp.

'*Exactement*. In the public dining room of my hotel. It will be very *comme il faut, je vous assure*.' There were undertones to his voice, but she could not identify them. She was focussing on the words.

He had used '*vous*' to her. The formal mode of address, implying not familiarity or superiority—but courtesy.

A knot inside her that she hadn't even been aware of untied itself.

But another one still remained. One that was much harder to untie. Impossible.

She should go home. She should not do this. If she wasn't working, she should be at home.

Because there was no point, no point at all, in having dinner with this man.

But it would be worth it if only for the memory.

She took a breath—and made her decision. Looking straight at him.

'Thank you,' she said. '*Il me fait un grand plaisir de vous accepter, m'sieu,*' she enunciated carefully. Then she looked at him uncertainly. 'Was that correct?' she asked.

His mouth quirked. Tension seemed to have gone out of his face.

'It will do perfectly,' he said.

He relaxed back into his seat, his shoulders easing.

'Where did you learn French?'

'At school,' she volunteered. She, too, sat back into the contours of the seat. 'Same as everyone else, really. I can just about get my way around France, but that's all. I can't really have a proper conversation, or read novels or watch TV or anything demanding. It always seems a bit bad, really, that the British— and the Americans, too, I suppose—can get away without knowing another language fluently. English is *de rigueur*, presumably, in business circles outside France?'

She was babbling, she knew, but it seemed important to her somehow to have an innocuous conversation—one that had nothing to do with where she worked, or what she'd thought he'd hired her for. A conversation she could have had with anyone.

'English now is very much the *lingua franca*, it's true, but I also speak Italian, Spanish, and some German, as well.'

Her reply was another burble.

'Well, I can say *café con leche, por favor* in Spanish, and *dov'e il cattedrale* in Italian, and I think that's about it. As for German, it's just *Bitte* and *Danke*. Oh, and I can say *epharisto* in Greek. But that's really my lot.' She gave a self-deprecating smile.

The long eyelashes swept down over his dark eyes. There were no more raindrops on them, but his hair was still clearly wet. So was hers. She could feel water trickling down her back. Another thought struck her. She could hardly dine in a hotel restaurant looking like a drowned rat. But maybe there would be powerful hand dryers in the Ladies, and she could at least get her hair dry. She could try and style it a bit, too, though it was probably best left in a tight pleat. But she could put a bit of make-up on, though—she had enough in her handbag after all. It was the clothes that were the main problem, however. She was just

wearing jeans and a jumper—would that really do? Well, it would have to. Anyway, her thoughts raced on, it obviously didn't bother him, or he wouldn't have asked her out in the way he had.

Why had he?

The question stung through her thoughts, scattering them instantly. Then into her head his words sounded. *Don't you ever look in the mirror?*

A quiver went through her. Was she really the kind of woman a man like him was interested in? She knew she could look good—knew she had been blessed with a face and figure that many women would envy her for. But a man like Xavier Lauran, rich, sophisticated and French, would move in circles where every woman was beautiful and chic, groomed from top to toe in exquisite designer clothes.

Doubt trickled through her. Then she put it aside. A man like Xavier Lauran would know his own mind. If he thought her beautiful enough to interest him, then that was that. He had, after all, no other reason to spend his time with her.

A warm glow began to spread through her. It might only be dinner, but in the evening ahead she would enjoy all she could of it.

She gave a silent mental shrug. Even if she had to do it in jeans and a jumper.

Fifteen minutes later, she realised she'd got that bit as wrong as everything else about the evening. She was being ushered across the huge, marble-floored lobby of a West End hotel, and guided distinctly towards the left-hand side.

'The hotel boutique is still open—I am sure they will have something suitable for you there.'

Lissa stopped dead, and looked round at Xavier Lauren.

'I beg your pardon?'

He glanced down at her. 'I don't wish to be critical, but you're soaking wet—as am I. And there is, I believe, a dress code at the

restaurant here that precludes jeans. So it would be a good idea to avail yourself of the resources of the hotel boutique.'

Lissa swallowed. 'I'm afraid I can't afford to buy anything there.'

'But I can—'

She shook her head. A quick, decisive action. 'Monsieur Lauran, I don't let men buy me clothes.'

He went on looking at her a moment.

'Consider it merely a loan. You can change back into your jeans at the end of the evening.'

'We could always eat somewhere where there's no dress code,' she ventured. 'There are loads of restaurants around here.'

'But I have made a reservation at this one. The chef is very good here. He is a Frenchman, you see. I make it a rule in London only to eat where the chef is French. That way I can protect my digestive system.'

There was deliberate humour in Xavier Lauran's voice.

'I can think of a number of British celebrity chefs who'd chop you up with meat cleavers for that comment,' Lissa was driven to retaliate. But the exchange had lightened the moment.

'Then you can see exactly why I prefer to dine in safety. Now, will you really not agree to my suggestion about the use of the hotel boutique?'

Lissa threw up her hands. 'OK—but I'm really not comfortable with it, you know.'

Something flickered at the back of his eyes. She couldn't tell what it was. But then she was more focussed on wondering, for the thousandth time, just how incredible it was just to look at him.

'*Bon,*' he said decisively. '*Alors—*' He continued to guide her into the boutique. 'Why don't you choose something and meet me in, say…' he shot back his cuff to glance at the thin gold watch around his lean wrist '…twenty minutes in the cocktail lounge.' He cast her a wry look. 'I myself have to dry out, as well.' He glanced at the shop assistant hovering not just atten-

tively but positively eagerly, Lissa noticed, but she could hardly blame the woman for her reaction. 'I am sure it will prove possible to provide suitable facilities for changing?'

'Certainly, sir,' said the other woman, and cast him a warm smile. 'If madam would like to see our collection?' Her eyes flickered down to Lissa's booted feet. 'And perhaps our footwear, too?'

'Whatever is necessary. Charge it all to my room.' He gave the number. Then he glanced back at Lissa. *'A bientôt,'* he said, and left her to it.

He strode off across the foyer towards the bank of lifts and headed up to his suite. He needed to shed his still-damp clothes, then shower and change. He also needed time.

Time to think straight. Think straight about Lissa Stephens— because Lissa Stephens was rearranging everything inside his head yet again, and he needed to make sense of it. Had to. Urgently. As he stood under the stinging needles of hot water, splintering on his back with the full punishing force of the hotel's water pressure, he knew that yet again Lissa Stephens had behaved against expectations. It had been shock enough to his system to discover, last night, that out of make-up and hostess costume she looked nothing like the money-grabbing tramp he had initially taken her to be. But now he had something else to make sense of.

Lissa Stephens had thought he'd booked her like a call girl— and she had gone ballistic. Why? Was it because she was too clever to be that unsubtle? Or was it because she had genuine objections to that kind of assumption? And she'd also objected to his assumption that he would provide her with an appropriate outfit for the evening.

His eyes narrowed as he turned off the water and stepped out, reaching for a towel to pat himself swiftly dry.

What game was Lissa Stephens playing?

Was she playing one at all?

Another question seared over the first.

Was it one she played, or didn't play, with all men?

Or only him?

With an impatient rasp he tossed the towel back on the vanity unit and stared at his reflection.

He knew his own attraction. Women were easy to attract—he had, after all, a potent combination they liked. His looks, his wealth, his position in society. Lissa Stephens might not be aware of the third, but she was certainly aware of the first two. Was that why she was giving her time to him? His eyes hardened suddenly. What if he only possessed the second of those attributes—wealth? Would she be here now, adorning herself downstairs, if he were not a wealthy man?

And was that the main attraction his brother held for her?

He needed to get her measure. It was essential. Imperative.

Then, like a punch to his stomach, he realised he already had it. Why would a woman having an affair with Armand be here, tonight, with another man—unless Armand meant nothing to her? Certainly not enough to stop her having dinner with another man.

But was dinner with another man crime enough in itself? Another thought spiked through his mind. What had she said when she was going ballistic at him in that damn rain? Something about getting fired if she didn't take the private hire for the evening? Was that why she'd agreed to his invitation to dinner? To keep her job?

Hell—he turned away from the mirror. He still couldn't get a steer on the girl. Every time he tried to nail her down, apply all the rational powers of his mind to her, the evidence slithered away from him again. With another muttered imprecation he strode through into the bedroom and started to get dressed.

His mood was not good. Damn Armand. Damn Lissa Stephens. Damn having to go through this rigmarole of finding out whether the girl was or wasn't fit to marry his brother.

And damn most of all, he thought, tight-lipped, as he finished knotting a silk tie at his throat and slipping on his suit jacket, the fact that right now the thought that was uppermost in his mind was just what Lissa Stephens would look like with a decent outfit on.

He slid his wallet and key into the inner pocket of his jacket, punched the lights, and set off to find out.

All thoughts of Armand seemed suddenly very far away, but right now he didn't care. Right now there was room for only one person in his thoughts. A girl he couldn't make out.

But whose measure it was essential he got—whatever it took.

CHAPTER FIVE

LISSA SAT, perched on the edge of a leather tub chair, her pulse too rapid, her breathing too shallow. Nervously, she tried to ease the tight material across her knees, but there was no give in it the way she was sitting, legs slanted sideways. Her spine was very straight. Across the scoop of her dress at the back she could feel the fall of her hair grazing lightly as she moved her head to keep the entrance to the cocktail lounge in view. She didn't look around, because if she did she knew she would catch the eyes of other men present, looking at her. They'd looked at her as she'd walked in, minutes ago, her nervous state making her hyper-aware of their glances. The glances, too, of other women present, checking her out, assessing her.

She knew what they were seeing—another woman like them, looking the way a woman should in a swanky place like this, with its soft lights and softer music emanating from the grand piano in one corner, and the retro-style bar winding sinuously along one wall, staffed by an abundance of barmen.

She'd never been in a place like this before. Before, in her earlier existence, when she'd dressed up to go out it had always been to places that were within her budget, or those of the men taking her out. None of them would have stretched to a swish five-star hotel like this. Here, the clientele was predominantly

male, all wearing business suits, or the occasional less-formal-but-still-expensive-looking casual wear.

A waiter came up to her, attentively asking her what she would like to drink.

'Oh, mineral water. Sparkling, please. Um, thank you,' she got out. Silently, she hoped Xavier Lauran was intending to show up. She didn't like to think what even mineral water cost in a place like this. More than she'd want to pay, certainly. The waiter returned almost instantly, but there was nothing so unsubtle as a tab accompanying the bottle and glass, with its sliver of lemon and chunks of ice, and the little bowl of expensive dry nuts set down on the small round table in front of her.

Nervously, she took a sip of the water poured out for her, then set the glass down again, still staring at the entrance. Twenty minutes was up—she'd rushed to make it on time. Rushed through the process of accepting the first dress that the woman in the boutique had proferred, and shoes and stockings to go with it, then being directed to the lavish Ladies' Cloakroom where there was ample room not just to change, but to do her make-up and style her rain-wet hair courtesy of the hairdyer the attendant had provided for her.

She took another sip of water and contemplated whether to start on the nuts. But she didn't want to get her fingers salty.

Her nerves jangled. She didn't let herself think. Didn't let herself think about what she was doing. Too late to change her mind now. And besides, she couldn't. The heavy truth of it was unavoidable. Being here, tonight, was the way she was going to keep the job she didn't want, but needed to keep.

And she wanted the memory, too. Just the memory. Of an evening spent with the most debonair man she had ever met—an evening far removed from the responsibilities of her everyday life. A daydream that just this one night was a reality.

And, oh, the reality.

He was walking into the lounge. She saw him instantly.

Her stomach hollowed. Faintness drummed in her ears. He was walking towards her, coming closer.

His eyes had gone to her. Seeing her as instantly as she had seen him. And in those eyes was something that simply sent her reeling.

It was a punch to his guts. He could feel it impacting. Like a fist. Blasting right through him.

He went on walking towards her, but he had absolutely no awareness of his surroundings. His entire focus was on the woman he was walking to. The woman who was blasting a hole right through him.

She looked—breathtaking. Stunning. Incredible.

Every last gram of speculation he'd entertained about just what she might look like when she had the right clothes, the right make-up and hairstyle, was confirmed. In spades.

His rapid expert gaze took in the whole package at a single glance. Hair—sleek, long, blow-dried back off her face. Face— every pure, perfect line set off by make-up that was simply another universe away from the garish layers she used at the casino. Now, subtle shadows accentuated the luminosity of her eyes, contoured her cheekbones, and then, finally, a rich sheen of lipstick perfectly delineated the delicate but sensuous curve of her mouth.

As for the dress—he gave a silent salute to the boutique saleswoman. Or was it Lissa Stephens herself who'd chosen that simple, but superbly cut coffee-coloured sleeveless silk shift that went so perfectly with her fair colouring? He didn't know, didn't care. Knew only that at last he was seeing Lissa Stephens as he had wanted to see her from the moment he had got out of the car the night before to offer her a lift home after purposely preventing her from catching her bus.

Why had he done that? Stopped her getting her bus so he could offer her a lift? He'd had a good reason, but right now he

didn't recall exactly why. There wasn't room inside his head for that. For anything. Anything at all except to close in, the way he was doing, on the woman sitting there as he walked up to her. He stopped dead in front of her, looking down.

'*Incroyable.*'

His voice was a husk. It turned Lissa inside out and back again. Her lips parted as she tilted her head to gaze up at him.

'*Incroyable,*' he murmured again. His eyes were washing over her, full force, working over every iota of her appearance, sweeping down over her, then back up again, to hold her own helpless, breathless gaze.

'I knew you would look good, but this….this is beyond all my expectations.'

For one moment longer his eyes held hers in that incredible, heart-stopping gaze, and then suddenly, like a switch going on, he smiled. She reeled again.

Gracefully, he lowered his lean frame into the adjacent chair, without taking his eyes off her. Immediately, claiming his attention in the most unobtrusive fashion, was the waiter who had served her. As Xavier Lauran's eyes left her, she felt at last the air returning to her lungs. Then, a moment later, with the waiter disappearing, it left them again. Xavier Lauran turned back to her.

'You look simply fantastic,' he told her. His voice was warm, and melting. Melting through her like honey.

She couldn't say anything. She was bereft of words. She had known in the first moment of seeing him, when he'd walked into the casino last night, that this man was like none she had ever known. But until this moment the full force of his power to render her breathless and helpless had not been turned on her. Now it was. Now, in a heady, incredible rush to her head, she knew that for the first time he was responding to her, and that responsiveness was making his own attractiveness totally lethal.

What was happening to her?

It was a pointless question. She knew with every shimmering cell in her body that what was happening to her now was making her reaction to him of the night before seem like the palest shadow of awareness.

It was like being carried away on a flood-tide—a flood-tide of heady awareness that was making her feel weightless and floating. Floating towards a destination she had no control over.

'Your champagne, sir,' said a voice.

She started, realising that the waiter had returned, and that he was bearing a tray with a bottle of champagne nesting in an ice bucket, smoky fumes curling from its opened neck. She watched as he carefully poured a little into one of the flutes on the tray, then proffered it to Xavier Lauran, who inhaled the bouquet and took a considering mouthful.

He nodded, and the waiter proceeded to pour out her glass, then fill the remainder of the other one. Then he was gone. Xavier picked up her flute and offered it to her, retaining his own. She took hers gingerly.

'*Salut.*' He clinked his glass against hers.

She took a sip simultaneously with him, then lowered the glass. Xavier glanced at her. 'A little better than last night's, *non?*' he said. There was amused irony in his voice, and in the lift of his eyebrow.

A smile broke from her. 'It's not even champagne, is it? What they serve there?'

'*Méthode champenoise,*' he agreed, with all the disdain of a Frenchman, for sparkling wine produced anywhere but in the élite Champagne region of France. 'And atrociously done at that. This, however, is champagne. Not one of the most famous houses, but all the better for that, I believe. And this is a particularly good vintage.' He took another savouring mouthful.

So did Lissa. 'It's gorgeous,' she said. Then she made a face. 'I'm sorry—that's a crass thing to say. I don't know anything

about champagne, I'm afraid—I only know that what they serve up at the casino is pretty grim. As well as being a hideous rip-off, of course. But I can tell this is completely different.' She frowned slightly. 'What makes it so good?'

'Many things. The grapes, the soil, the weather, the slope, and above all the nose of the *chef du cave,* whose responsibility it is to ensure the quality of the *assemblage*—the blending of the grapes which gives each champagne its distinctive character.'

Xavier leaned back in his chair, the flute held carefully in his fingers. They were long fingers. Lissa's eyes went to them, and for the briefest moment she had a vision of their tips just touching her face, even as they were touching the glass. She dragged her eyes away, making herself listen to what he was saying. He was explaining the factors that went into creating a vintage champagne—one that would be made from the grapes of one year's harvest alone, not blended with those from previous years. She listened attentively, interested in the subject as much as simply revelling in listening to his beautiful, accented voice, revelling in his attention being focussed on her.

'What are *crus?*' she asked. 'I've never understood those, either.'

Xavier enlightened her.

It was good to talk about something like champagne. He could talk without thinking, and that was good right now. He didn't want to think. He wanted to watch. He wanted to watch the way Lissa Stephens held her champagne glass with a natural grace and elegance, the way she lifted it to her mouth from time to time, and the way her soft lips embraced the lip of the flute. He wanted to watch her gazing across at him, her eyes hanging on his, deep and smoky. He wanted—

'Your table is ready now, sir, if you would like to go through?'

The *maître d'* from the adjacent restaurant was hovering deferentially. Xavier nodded. He got to his feet.

'Shall we?' he invited Lissa.

She stood up. She didn't feel quite steady on her feet, but it had nothing to do with the champagne she'd been sipping.

And everything to do with the man she was about to dine with.

Supremely self-consciousness of his scrutiny, she walked forward into the dining room. The shoes that went with the dress were a fraction tight, but she didn't care. She only knew the dress itself made her feel like a million dollars, moulding her body and yet simultaneously skimming her contours. She let the *maître d'* show them to their table, secluded and private on the far side of the dining room, and took her place on the banquette with the same self-consciousness.

The business of ordering food—a lengthy process, involving no less a personage than the chef himself, emerging from his domain to conduct an intensive, mutually satisfactory conversation in rapid, idiomatic French with this man for whom any chef would proffer his arts and skills—helped her relax. So, too, did the continued sips of champagne. She wasn't entirely sure how much she'd drunk, because her glass never seemed to be empty. She would need to be careful, she knew, but only with an abstract part of her mind.

Prudence, caution, being sensible—all seemed qualities that had nothing to do with what was happening to her now.

Because what was happening to her now was magic. Pure and simple.

Magic to sit here at the same table as this man, the man who could turn her inside out and back again with a single long-lashed glance. Magic to be so wonderfully, shiveringly aware of what he was doing to her. Magic to listen to his smooth, deliciously accented voice, talking about…well, she couldn't really think what. But it was easy, undemanding conversation that flowed between them, back and forth, on easy, undemanding topics, and yet she knew, with that same breathless awareness, that it was simply a vehicle for a conversation that was taking

place far below the level of her consciousness—a conversation that had one subject only.

Unspoken, but there—in every glance, in every moment her eyes were held by his, in her every helpless gaze.

The exquisite meal seemed to go on for ever, yet was over in a flash. And then, somehow, she was sipping a tiny *demi-tasse* of coffee, whose intensity of aroma was almost as heady as the wines she had drunk. Too many wines, too much. But she didn't care. They had served only to exquisitely enhance the headiness lifting her which had nothing to do with alcohol or caffeine.

And everything to do with the man sitting opposite her.

The conversation died away. Around them, the rest of the diners were leaving. The room was nearly empty. The buzz of conversation all around had ebbed. The emptiness of the dining room seemed to throw a web of even greater privacy around them.

More than privacy.

Intimacy.

She felt it like a tangible brush of silk across her skin. It made her feel as if she were caught in a cocoon, cradling her, embracing her.

She gazed across at Xavier. She wasn't sure at what point he had become Xavier, but now he was.

Xavier—she let the syllables of his name flow silently, caressingly, through her mind. Just as she was letting the warmth of his gaze caress her. She let her eyes mingle with his, let herself look deep into those beautiful, dark eyes that were looking back at her, looking at her in a way that was slowly, very slowly, dissolving her from the inside.

She knew its name. Had always known its name.

But now—now she felt its power. Power that she had never known.

Till now.

Her hands at her coffee cup stilled. She saw his hand move

across the damask surface of the tablecloth. Saw, as if in slow motion, his hand reach for hers.

And touch. Touch with those long, sensitive fingers that she had watched cradle the golden flute of champagne. Now they were devastatingly cradling her fingers, turning her hand over so that her fingers were resting on his square, strong palm.

She felt a thousand feathering sensations in every millimetre that he touched.

His eyes held hers.

For an endless moment he did not speak. The whole world was this moment, this sensation.

Then, in a low, husky voice, he said what she had both longed to hear him say—and dreaded.

'I want you very much. Will you stay with me tonight?'

He had said it. Beneath the low murmur of his voice, emotions surged like a flood-tide in him.

All evening he had felt the tide running. Running strong and silent and so powerful that its strength all but overwhelmed him. Where had it come from, this overpowering tide that was sweeping through him? Sweeping away things he must not let it sweep away.

He tried to drag those things back, because he must not let them be lost, but the tide was running stronger and stronger still.

He knew its name. Had felt its power before. But never like this.

He tried to fight it. But it was like swimming against a current so strong that he could make no headway. Nor did he want to fight it. That was the worst—that knowledge, that grim recognition deep inside him, that what he was doing now was not what he had planned to do.

It should not have come to this. He should have stopped it, halted it in its tracks, forced it by main strength back down into the subterranean depths of his being where it belonged.

But he couldn't—and now, unstoppable, incurable, it had taken the ascendant. Brought him to this moment.

His eyes held hers, his hand had taken hers, and now nothing else mattered.

Except one thing.

The answer to his question.

He saw her eyes flare. Her lips part.

And then, like a long, slow exhalation, he heard her speak.

'I can't…'

For a moment he was still—quite still. Then, his eyes never leaving hers, never letting hers go for an instant, a second, he spoke, too.

'Why not?'

His fingers, without conscious volition on his part, had tightened around hers.

Her eyes were huge, haunted. Haunting.

'I can't,' she said again. Her voice was a thread of breath. 'I have…' She swallowed, and for a moment her face was stark and bleak. 'Commitments.'

'There is someone else?' He spoke sharply, like a knife cutting.

The moment of truth now. Truth on so many points. All of them impaling him.

Slowly, she nodded. 'Yes. Someone very important to me.'

He let go her hand. Forsaking it as if suddenly it were a poisonous snake. His jaw tightened.

'And yet,' he said, clipping out each word, harsh and hard, 'you chose to dine with me tonight?'

She bit her lip. He could see it, and it sent a punishing flare through him to see the whiteness of her teeth indent into the soft curve of tender flesh.

'I…I had to.' She was forcing the words out, he could see, her eyes still wide and huge. 'I told you—'

His eyes narrowed. Something in her face was pinched suddenly.

'Ah, yes, your charming employers—threatening you with—what is that clumsy English expression? Ah, yes—threatening you with the sack if you did not accept my invitation to dinner.'

She'd slipped her hand from the table.

'Yes,' she said in a small voice. Her eyes would not meet his.

He got to his feet. It was an abrupt, sudden movement.

'I regret, then, *mademoiselle*, that I have so mistaken the situation. Permit me, if you will, to offer you my apologies for having done so. And now allow me to place my car at your disposal. Feel free to be driven either to your place of employment or to your home, and, of course, to your "very important someone".'

He gave a curt nod of his head and walked away.

Fury blasted through him. Blind, explosive fury. A white rage behind his eyes, obliterating everything.

It was irrational, deranged, insane.

He knew it was—knew it and didn't care. Didn't care as he strode out of the restaurant and across the marbled foyer to the bank of lifts. He punched the button savagely.

He wanted out.

Damn her. Damn her to hell for what she'd done. Letting him get sucked, deeper and deeper, into that running tide. Gazing at him like that all evening, sending her message to him as loud and clear as if she were using a PA system. Sitting there looking so extraordinarily beautiful that it had taken all his strength, all evening, not to reach out for her.

And then, when he had, she'd turned him down.

The fury blitzed in him again. She'd turned him down. Said no. No.

A single word.

Denying him what he wanted.

Her.

Because that was what he wanted—he wanted her. He wanted

her now—right now—tonight. He wanted her to be here, her hand enclosed in his, waiting to step inside the lift, the lift that would be closed and private... And he would turn her to him, and slide his hands around that slender, pliant waist, and slant his mouth down over her soft, sensuous lips and taste, taste the sweetness she would offer.

He would mould her body to his, feel the ripe mound of the breasts that he'd been seeing all evening, and would have the exquisite sensation of their pressure against his hard, muscled torso. His hands would shape her spine, fingers splaying out, reaching to the delicate, sensitive nape of her neck, while his mouth played sensuously, arousingly, with hers.

He felt his body tightening, felt the tide that had been running stronger and stronger all evening reach that *point non plus* that was unbearable to endure—all courtesy of one, single word.

No.

The lift doors sliced open as the lift arrived, and he stepped forward.

And halted.

He frowned, struck by a memory.

'No' had not been the word she had used. She had used a quite different word.

Slowly his hand came up to halt the doors closing again, forcing them back with unnoticed strength so that they juddered apart. Then he stepped back onto the marble floor.

Lissa Stephens hadn't said no to him. She had said, 'I can't.'

He stilled. Slowly, the white rage of frustration and denial and the fury born of something he knew he had to push aside drained from him.

All logic, all reason had left him—swept away on that tide. He took a harsh, heavy breath, standing immobile by the lift. That tide which had swept away everything else except the single, overriding imperative of the evening.

But that hadn't been the purpose of this evening. This evening had been about something quite different.

Emotion drained from him to be replaced by bleak, belated recognition. In his head sounded yet again the low, strained sound of her voice.

'I can't…'

And she had said exactly why that was so. Because of the existence of *'someone very important to me.'*

Like a squad of booted soldiers the words marched back inside his head from which that swirling, overpowering tide had swept them. But they were back now, with their heavy, booted tread that trampled on anything and everything in their way.

Logic, reason, sense.

With bleak, controlled acquiescence he let them in.

Lissa Stephens had turned him down. Turned him down because she had commitments elsewhere to someone 'very important' to her. And that someone was Armand. And that she had turned him, Xavier, down tonight meant only one thing—Lissa Stephens's loyalty was to his brother.

Did she love Armand? Was her commitment to him out of love, or because a rich man was offering her marriage? Offering her an escape from the casino, from that squalid place she lived, from the poverty of her life?

He didn't know. He couldn't know.

For all that he had found out about her, for all the time he had spent with her, talked with her, she was still a mystery—a contradiction. A woman possessed of rare beauty, as well as—so his conversation with her this evening had amply demonstrated—clear intelligence. And yet she chose to work where she did. Was prepared to make herself look like a tart night after night, and yet had walked out of her job when she was required to do anything more than look like one. A woman who accepted an invitation to dine with him, a wealthy man—and yet who refused to let him

buy her a dress to go with the invitation. A woman who gazed deep into his eyes as if she were prepared to drown herself in them—and yet who said 'I can't' when it came to anything more.

Well, he thought, with a bitter, bleak weariness, it was his turn to say *I can't*.

He could do no more. He accepted it. He had done everything in his power to discover the true worth, or lack thereof, of the woman his brother said he wanted to marry.

A hollowing, savage humour stabbed through him. But it had no humour in it—only a bleak, bitter irony that cut to the very quick of him. In the end he had discovered only one thing about her that he knew to be true. And it was a knowledge that mocked him.

Cursed him.

As it would curse any man who shared his fate, a fate he would wish on no man, but which had fallen upon himself.

Because the one, overwhelming truth that he knew about Lissa Stephens was that he desired her. Wanted her.

For himself.

The woman his brother wanted to marry.

Forbidden desire.

A curse from hell itself.

CHAPTER SIX

LISSA sat at the table, very still. The champagne, the wine, all the magic of the evening had drained out of her, emptying out of her like water down a well.

She hadn't thought it would be like this. So brutal.

But then—she gave a twist to her mouth—she hadn't thought at all, had she?

She'd sat here, floating on air, entranced by the magic of the evening, and had never thought of how it must end.

Because she hadn't wanted it to end. She knew that this was all there could be, and she hadn't wanted it to end, had wanted it to go on for ever and ever.

But it hadn't. Of course it hadn't. This had been a time out, that was all, a brief, magical time out. A gift that would at the stroke of midnight dissolve, leaving nothing behind but memories.

She felt her throat tighten. She had known the evening would end, but not like this.

She heard again, *felt* again, the savage civility of his voice, felt his absolute repudiation of her, dropping her hand as if it were rotting meat.

Did he have to be so brutal?

She felt tears prick in the back of her eyes and blinked, angry with herself.

Oh, come on. Wise up. Why the Little Miss Sensitive act suddenly? she berated herself. He'd said 'dinner', but obviously he'd had more in mind than that, and he hadn't liked being turned down. Men never liked being turned down—and a man like him probably never had been. That was why he'd stormed off like that. She'd caught him in the most delicate part of male anatomy: his ego.

Her face puckered. But he wasn't like that. He hadn't been all evening. He had been wonderful. Attentive, charming, engaging, with that dry, ironic humour that brought a glint to his eye and a smile to her mouth. He had been the perfect dinner companion, and as for everything else—well, that had just been magic, the only word for it.

Until that brutal departure. Her throat tightened again, and she took a jerky sip of cooling coffee, forcing it down to try and open her throat.

It had been so out of place, that flare of icy anger. She took a painful breath. Surely a man as sophisticated, as obviously experienced with women as he was, could have managed the scene more gracefully? Even if he'd smarted at her rebuff, he need not have shown it—he could have extricated himself with élan, with a smooth word, affecting regret, with sophistication and charm. But he hadn't. Obviously when it came to bedtime, Xavier Lauran, for all his cool sophistication, all the seductive magic of his eyes, his voice, was just another man who thought the price of a meal included a woman for the night.

He'd promised her 'just dinner' and like a fool she'd believed him.

She slid out from her seat. Presumably the waiting staff would take care of petty concerns like the bill, and although there was someone instantly there to help pull the table back sufficiently and bid her good-night, she knew it was pretty obvious that her escort had stormed out on her. Well… She gave a silent, heavy sigh. What was that to her? Nothing. Just as it was nothing that

Xavier Lauran had proved, after all, to be a man who for all his expensive packaging still operated on the same sordid, commercial premise that any of the punters at the casino did when they thought they could indulge in some 'private hire' with the hostesses.

The only difference was, they were more honest about it.

She walked out of the restaurant, head held high.

She needed to change. Her own clothes had been put in another bag from the shop, and she'd checked it in to the Ladies' Cloakroom. They would be damp still, she knew, but it didn't matter. What mattered was getting out of here. If the boutique was closed, she'd simply put the dress, stockings and shoes neatly folded inside the original bags, and leave them with the concierge to be given to Xavier Lauran. What he did with them she didn't care. Hand them on to the next stupid female he wanted to have for dinner…and breakfast.

Not, of course, that breakfast was necessarily on the menu. Who knew? Maybe he just chucked them out after he'd had sex with them and sent them home in his damn chauffeur-driven car. Maybe they were OK with that sort of treatment. Maybe Xavier Lauran deliberately picked up girls like he'd clearly thought her to be, cheap hostesses in cheap casinos, because he knew they'd be so impressed by him, by his flash car and his offer of dinner cooked by a French chef, and the free run of a five-star hotel boutique. Maybe Xavier Lauran deliberately—

'Lissa—'

She stalled, head whipping around. He was heading towards her, walking from the bank of lifts. His stride was rapid, intent on intercepting her. She started forward again, her pace increasing urgently. She had to get to the Ladies. It would be sanctuary. Safety. Safe from Xavier Lauran, who'd smiled so devastatingly into her eyes and who'd only wanted a night of sex with her.

She made it to the Ladies, hurling herself inside and then

standing there trembling. She dived into a stall and plonked herself down on the closed unit. She stared at the locked door.

Her mouth pressed together.

Truth pressed down on her.

Oh, God, what a hypocrite she was. She could rant away all she liked about men thinking that dinner meant bed-and-breakfast, as well, and get on her high horse that Xavier Lauran was no better than any of them. But she knew, as she swallowed through the tight, stricken cords in her throat, that, berate him all she might, the truth was that she was a hypocrite. A one hundred per cent, fully paid-up hypocrite.

She made herself say the words. Say them clearly and plainly in her head.

I would have said yes.

If she could have, she would have said yes.

She closed her eyes, sinking down her head. She would have done it. She would have let him take her by the hand, lead her upstairs, let him take her into his arms, slide his mouth across hers to take the possession of it the way she had wanted right from the very first moment she saw him, let him take possession of her body.

For however long he wanted. For a single hour, a single night—however long he wanted her.

That was his power. That was the power she had felt flowing into her, through her, unstoppable, unavoidable. The power of an emotion that she had never felt before, but which she now felt more intensely, more overwhelmingly than she knew she would ever feel about any man again.

The power of desire.

Her eyes shadowed, and she lifted her face from her hands.

Desire she could never fulfil.

Because it was impossible, just impossible. Nothing in her life made it possible for her to say what she had longed to be able to say, that simple, sighing *yes*.

She stiffened her spine. Well, it was just as well she hadn't, wasn't it? Just as well she'd said, 'I can't.' Because that had unleashed a side of Xavier Lauran he'd hidden from her all evening, ever since he'd denied buying her time for what the casino had sold it to him for.

Anger spurted through her. She was glad of it. Grateful. It helped to scour out the stupid, naïve mush that was making her hide herself away like this. It was as well she'd got the measure of the man, so she could see the 'magic' for what it was. For him nothing more than a ritual to be gone through before moving on to the main event of the evening. And when he was denied it he'd turned nasty.

With a heavy, hard heart, she got to her feet. She had to get out of here. She had to get changed and go home, back to her real life. She went out into the washroom area, collecting her bag of clothes from the cloakroom, then retired back into the cubicle to change. The jeans were still damp, but tough. Her jacket would keep her warm enough, and it was still early enough to travel by Tube, which would be warmer. She'd go straight home, not back to work. She couldn't face it—not tonight. Would Xavier Lauran complain about her to the casino manager? Consider himself short-changed because she hadn't come across for him, even after all the soft soaping he'd given her? Well, too bad. She'd assumed she was out of a job when she'd left the casino this evening—so if she was, she was.

Leaving a tip for the attendant she could ill afford, she headed out of the Ladies. The beautiful silk dress was folded back into its tissue paper, the shoes nestling in the base of the bag, stockings neatly wrapped. No one would want to wear them, obviously, but they belonged to Xavier Lauran. He'd paid for them, and he would get them back, along with the rest of what he'd dolled her up in.

She glanced warily around as she marched towards the concierge's desk, but there was no sign of him. Good—he'd left.

She clumped heavily on the marble floor, and didn't care. She reached the concierge and hefted up the boutique bags.

'For Mr Xavier Lauran,' she said shortly. 'I don't know his room number.'

'Certainly, madam,' the uniformed concierge said, and lowered the bags behind his desk. She nodded her thanks, and headed to the main entrance of the hotel. The revolving doors opened on to a portico where taxis and cars could draw up. Was Xavier Lauran's chauffeured car still waiting for her? She didn't care if it was. She wasn't getting into it anyway. There was a Tube station quite near here, and the rain had stopped finally. It was chilly, but dry. She wanted to go home.

She hovered on the exterior concourse a moment, getting her bearings. She was somewhere in Mayfair, on the corner of one of the grand Georgian squares, but for a moment her orientation was awry. She glanced around.

And there was Xavier Lauran. Tall, hands plunged into the pockets of his cashmere overcoat. Immobile. Waiting.

He walked up to her. She tried to walk past him. He blocked her instantly, hands slipping from his pockets and catching her by her elbows.

'Lissa—please. If you do nothing else, let me apologise.'

She stared up at him.

'I behaved like a brute. An oaf. And I'm sorry—truly sorry.'

How he did it she didn't know, but he guided her to the far end of the concourse, where there were no people, no cars, no doorman.

He looked down at her. There was an expression in his eyes she hadn't seen before. It made him look…different. She didn't know why. Could only know, right now, that her heart had started to thump. With hard, heavy slugs.

And that her throat was tight, so tight.

'I'm truly sorry,' he said again, and his voice was different, too, though she couldn't tell why.

He was speaking again, and she forced herself to listen over the pounding of her heart.

'If there is someone else in your life, then I understand. And I respect you for being honest with me—and I am sorry, truly, for having placed you in this position in the first place. Making you feel that you had to accept my invitation or risk your job—even though it's a job I wish you didn't have.' He took a breath. It seemed ragged to her ears.

'I told you I was merely inviting you for dinner, and you have my word that at the time that is all I intended. Nothing more. But—' He took another indrawn breath. 'When I saw you, dressed as your beauty should be dressed, I was simply blown away. I have no other excuse. And I thought...' his eyes washed over her, and she felt her legs weaken. 'I thought you were responding to me in the same way, for the same reason.' His mouth pressed minutely, then released. 'Which is why I made the invitation that I did. I did not mean it insultingly or cheaply.'

His hands around her elbows eased upwards, and without her realising it he was drawing her closer to him.

'You are so beautiful,' he said softly. 'Even now, knowing as I do that you are not free, even with that knowledge I still want for this one, single time—this. Allow me, please—for it is all I can have of you.'

He lowered his head to hers.

His kiss was heaven. Soft, and lingering and exquisite. She gave herself to it, gave herself with all the yearning she was filled with to the magic in his lips, his touch, taken for those few precious moments to a paradise she had not known existed.

And then, even as her heart soared, he was drawing away from her, letting go of her.

'Goodbye,' he said softly.

And then he was walking away.

CHAPTER SEVEN

'I've got a booking for you at an insurance company.'

The temp agency girl's voice was brisk and businesslike. Lissa forced herself to concentrate. It was punishingly hard. For a start she was tired—but that was nothing new. Her late nights at the casino always left her tired. She should be grateful, though, that she still had a job there. She had so very nearly lost it.

But what was new, horribly, bleakly new, was this sense of the world having had all the colour drained out of it. Everything was grey.

Only one single place had colour in it—only one place was bathed in radiant, luminous light. Her memory of that evening—that precious, unforgettable evening which shone like a jewel in the secret, private place she kept it.

Yet it was a jewel with facets that were razor sharp, piercing her with pain whenever she permitted herself to remember that night.

But she had made the right decision—the only decision. There was nothing else she could have done.

Even as she told herself that, a small, treacherous voice would whisper in her inner ear.

You could have had one night...one hour...that, at least, you could have had...

But she knew she could not have done that. Knew that if she

had succumbed to that exquisite temptation, the pain she felt now would be nothing in comparison. One night, one hour in his bed, would have only created a longing in her for more that she could never assuage.

He was not for her. He couldn't be. She had duties and obligations elsewhere. Commitments.

And more, so much more than that—she had love. Love and responsibility and care. She couldn't abandon them. Not for a night, not for an hour, not for a minute.

But it was hard—however much she reminded herself that it was impossible to indulge her desire for the man who had, out of nowhere, suddenly transformed her life. She knew she had to forget him but the longing could not be suppressed. Only repressed. Shut down tightly into the box of 'might have beens.'

Well, there were a lot of 'might have beens' in her life. And they had all ended with that hideous, bloody mess of twisted metal and broken bodies.

Except *her* body.

Guilt, survivor guilt, seared through her. As she stood up from the chair in the agency, her legs strong and healthy, her body strong and healthy, she felt guilt go through her. Guilt and resolution.

Keep going—keep going. Work, by day and by night, work and earn and save.

But would she ever have enough?

Into her mind, the treacherous thought came again.

If only Armand...

But it had been days now, days after days, and nothing. Absolutely nothing.

Hope had drained out of her. Just as colour had drained out of her life.

She got to her feet, ready to set out for the insurance company's offices. At least temping gave her higher rates than per-

manent work, and it was flexible enough for her needs—like the days she had to get to the hospital.

Guilt stabbed her, as it always did whenever she fell into self-pity or resentment. She had no right whatsoever to either emotion.

She had walked out of the crash without a scratch.

In her mind's eye formed, as it always did, the image that haunted her, tormented her. The hospital chapel, the two cold, still bodies.

And one more body, still alive, but broken, still broken.

Pain choked her. And guilt. Not just guilt for having walked out of the crash that had destroyed so much, but guilt now for wanting even more from life than what she already had.

Wanting Xavier Lauran.

Whom she could never have.

Xavier sat at his desk, his eyes resting on the unopened e-mail on his screen. It was from Armand. His expression tightened. He did not want to open the e-mail. Did not want to read it. He didn't want to think about Armand, and most of all he did not want to think about the woman his brother wanted to marry.

Not thinking about Lissa Stevens was essential. He had spent every day since that night at the hotel not thinking about her. He had spent every night battling not to remember her.

A bitter smile twisted his mouth. The saying was true—the road to hell *was* paved with good intentions. He'd had only good intentions when he'd made the decision to check out the woman Armand had talked about wanting to marry. His only thought then had been to save his brother from a disaster that, on past performance, was a real risk. But his good intentions had turned on him.

At some point he knew, with that cool, rational brain that he'd used to live his life by, he would have to think about Lissa Stephens. He would have to come to terms with the disaster that had befallen not his brother but himself. He had fallen, head first,

into a pit of his own making. A pit he could not escape but which he had to find a way of dealing with.

Just how he was going to deal with it, however, was at the moment completely beyond him. His eyes shadowed. He had wanted Lissa Stephens that fateful night with an intensity that had shocked him as much as it had enthralled him—and he still wanted her. Wanted her more than ever. She was a presence he could not rid himself of, a memory he could not burn out of his mind. Though he refused to let himself think of her, that did not mean she was not there.

He wanted her.

He wanted her, and he did not care that she worked in a casino, did not care that he still did not know whether she was or was not fit to marry his brother, did not care if she was going to marry his brother.

It did not stop him wanting her.

What was he going to do? How could he meet her again, on Armand's arm, and know that she was never going to be his?

The thought tormented him, the harsh, brutal knowledge that she was forbidden to him. Never before in his life had any woman he'd wanted been forbidden to him. He had never looked at married women, and none who were unmarried, with whom he'd decided to embark on a liaison, had ever turned him down. Why should they have? He had always been able to have the women he wanted. It had never been an issue, never been something he'd thought deeply about, never had cause to. He'd selected women from the many available to him with the same rationale he brought to bear on everything in his life. She would be beautiful, chic, well educated, well-bred, an *habituée* of the circles in which he moved. She would be experienced in the art of love, and she would want exactly what he wanted—a sensual, suitable sexual and social partner who would fit the space in his life which he allocated for that purpose. And when the affair lost its

flavour, as it always did at some point, then she would agree with him that it was time to part, without rancour or regret.

But now he had been given a poisoned chalice by fate.

I desire my brother's bride…

With tight, heavy emotion he clicked on Armand's e-mail. His eyes scanned the words rapidly. It was just about his upcoming business schedule in the USA. Nothing about marriage plans.

Why not?

The question hung in Xavier's focus. Why had Armand gone so quiet on a topic he'd written so enthusiastically about only a short time ago? Xavier's mouth tightened. Was Armand's reticence now because he did not trust his brother not to interfere, even though he'd asked him not to? Did he suspect that being despatched to the Middle East and America had been a deliberate ploy on his part?

A heavy rasp escaped Xavier. What did it matter? From now on he was out of it—he had to keep a very, very long distance from Armand and his plans to marry Lissa Stephens. It was the only safe thing to do—the only rational thing.

Lissa Stephens could never be his.

However much he wanted her.

It had been a long, tiring day, and Lissa had to force herself to walk briskly out of her local Tube station in the rush-hour crowds. She carried bags of grocery shopping bought from one of the City supermarkets. It meant lugging the bags home, but there was no supermarket near her flat—only a dingy convenience store near the entrance to the station, stocking overpriced groceries and sad looking fruit and vegetables. This part of London depressed her. Here in the tatty concrete wilderness around the Tube station, an unsuccessful urban regeneration project of the fifties and sixties, where the only people were those who could not afford anywhere better, her spirits never failed to droop.

But, however depressing the area, her flat did nevertheless have advantages. Not only was it social housing, so the rent was low for London, but it was also on the ground floor, and only a quarter of a mile away from St Nathaniel's Hospital, which made her mandatory weekly visits there blessedly easier.

Her expression changed slightly as she rebalanced her shopping bags and continued to trudge homeward in the dusk.

It had been on one of her weekly visits to St Nat's that she had first met Armand. He had been visiting a colleague who had collapsed with a heart attack, so he'd said later, but it had taken only a single look as they'd waited for the elevator together for him to smile, so warmly, so appreciatively.

And that was how it had started.

If only—

No. Automatically she cut off the pointless hope. There was no purpose in holding on to it. It was folly to hold out for the happy-ever-after ending that she dreamed of, where Armand's magic wand would make everything all right. In the end there was only herself to rely on. Even as she forced herself to recall that, a thought came to her.

Xavier…

Xavier Lauran is rich…

No.

It was impossible and out of the question. She must not let her thoughts stray in that dangerously tempting direction. She must not let her thoughts stray to him, period. Doing so was like poking a wound with a stick, just to see the blood run.

She reached the old Victorian tenement and got out her keys. Her spirits low, battered on all fronts, she told herself she had to keep on at the task ahead of her. She could do nothing else. All her strength, her focus, her time and her will-power, had to be bent to that purpose only.

Work, earn, save. No let up, no reprieve. For as long as it took.

As she opened the door to the flat, she froze. There were voices inside, and they were not coming from the television. One was familiar, but the tone was not familiar, at all. It was excited, happy, with no trace of either the thread of pain or the drug-induced slurring. The other voice was also familiar but hearing it made her surge disbelievingly into the living room and stop dead. A figure unfolded from the battered sofa. Lissa's face lit.

'Armand,' she cried.

She went into his outstretched arms.

'Xavier, have you been listening to anything I've said?'

The voice beside him was light, with a teasing note, but Xavier had to force himself to pay attention. He'd had to force himself to pay attention to everything that Madeline de Cerasse had said to him all evening. He'd taken her out to dinner. It had been a deliberate gesture on his part. Completely rational. He needed, he knew, to pick up his normal life. He needed, he knew even better, to have sex as soon as possible. With another woman. And since he was, he realised, technically still regarded as her lover, at least by her, he knew it would have to be Madeline.

There was only one problem. He had absolutely no desire whatsoever to take Madeline to bed.

His eyes rested on her a moment. Her beautifully styled brunette crop set off a face of piquant allure, matched by a chicly elegant body that she was well skilled in using to sensual advantage in bed. He had every reason to desire her.

Yet he did not. He did not want her.

He only wanted one woman.

And he couldn't have her.

Abruptly, knowing he was breaking his own first rule of *affaires* with his selected partners, he set down his fork. He was always considerate and tactful when the time came to end a re-lationship, letting his partner have sufficient time not just to

accustom herself to the dissolution of their affair, but also to arrange an alternative partner for herself, to make the parting easier. This time he was neither.

'I have something to say to you,' he announced brusquely.

Five minutes later he was sitting at the table on his own. Madeline had gone. He was not surprised. He had tried to soften the blow, but it had been difficult to do so at such short notice. She had reacted by assuming the role of offended woman. He had allowed her to do so, letting himself appear the brute it comforted her to cast him as.

Well, perhaps he *was* a brute. There was certainly anger burning in him. Anger at himself. He should not have interfered in his brother's life. He should have left his marriage plans well alone. He should have—

He tossed down his napkin and got to his feet abruptly. It was irrelevant what he should or should not have done. It was too late.

Too late for regrets. Too late for everything.

Lissa Stephens was not for him and never could be, and there was nothing, absolutely nothing, that he could do about it.

How could the world change so much, so swiftly? The question swirled in Lissa's head like a carousel, making her giddy with happiness. It had all happened so quickly—dizzyingly quickly. Armand had flown in from Dubai and done what Lissa had prayed that he would—and feared so much that he would not. He had waved his wonderful, miraculous magic wand and transformed everything. He had made all the necessary arrangements—that was what he'd been doing when he'd gone so quiet, so it would be a wonderful surprise, he'd said, his face lit from within with a glow that had made Lissa curl with happiness.

Now, a mere twenty-four hours later, it was done. America next stop.

She didn't mind being left behind—understood the reason for

it and rejoiced in it. As she made her way back from the airport even the damp and derelict street she lived in suddenly seemed bathed in glorious sunshine. Everything was radiant.

It took her another twenty-four hours, so suffused in happiness was she, for the realisation to come to her. When it did, her breath caught with the impact of it. She had three weeks to herself—the time the trip to America would take.

Three whole weeks.

Her breath stilled in her lungs.

A name distilled in her mind.

Xavier.

Do I dare? Do I really dare?

Her lips parted as she slowly exhaled.

Why should she not dare? She had three precious weeks to herself, and even a day, a single night, would be treasure more than she had ever thought to have.

A shadow fell across her face. But what if he no longer wanted her?

She'd probably been just a passing fancy—an impulse of the moment. Why should she have been anything else?

She told herself that in all probability Xavier Lauran, after accepting she would not spend the night with him, had simply returned to Paris and never given her another thought. For a man like him, with looks like his, there would be a queue around the block of women—all those beautiful, elegant, chic Parisiennes he was surrounded by—lining up to try and tempt him.

Yet a temptation of her own circled endlessly in her mind. What if he did still want her? And if he did, then now—now she had a golden opportunity. So, did she dare—did she really dare— get in touch with him?

Her stomach churned. It was not just a question of whether Xavier Lauran wanted her still. It was also a question of whether she really should go ahead and do this. Have an affair—a fling—

call it what she would—with Xavier Lauran. But even as the doubt voiced itself, a protesting cry seemed to come from deep within her. There would never, she knew, be another man like Xavier Lauran in her life! A man who could stop the breath in her body. Who turned her knees to jelly and set the blood racing in her veins. No, there would never be another man like him. Nor would an opportunity like this ever come again. This chance to have, even for a brief time, something she would remember all her life would never come twice. It was now or never.

She couldn't bear it to be never. She could tell herself all she liked that all she could have was a brief affair—a passing fling. Maybe only a single night. If that. But to let it go just for want of being brave enough to dare—she could not do that. Would not.

For another sleepless night she tossed and turned on it, wanting it so much, yet not daring to dare. All morning, as she did her work at the insurance company, she brooded on the number for the London branch of XeL she'd looked up. But did she dare, did she really dare, to phone him?

By the time she took her lunchbreak she was a bag of nerves. She took her mobile phone and went to the Ladies, forcing herself to key in the number.

How can I do this—phone him up and tell him…. Tell him I'm available…?

She almost cut the call—and then it was answered.

'XeL International, may I help you?'

For a moment Lissa's voice froze, then she made herself speak.

'Er—I'm trying to get in touch with Xavier Lauran.' Her heart was thumping like a hammer.

'Putting you through.' There was a pause, then another ring tone, sounding foreign. A woman answered, speaking French. Lissa completely failed to catch what she said. So she simply repeated what she'd said to the UK switchboard, sticking to English. There was a pause. An audible one. Then the woman spoke again, in English.

'What name, please?'

'Er— Lissa Stephens.' Lissa's voice was breathless with nerves. There was another pause. Then the woman spoke again. Smoothly and fluently.

'Monsieur Lauran is in conference. I'm so sorry.'

Lissa swallowed. 'Um— can I leave a message for him?'

'Of course.' The French-accented voice was as smooth as cream, but Lissa suddenly realised that she was simply being treated as someone to get off the line as soon as possible. Was Xavier really 'in conference' or just not available to women who phoned him out of the blue? But she wasn't going to hang up without at least doing what she'd been nerving herself to do all night and all morning.

'Thank you.' Her voice sounded strangulated, but she made herself go on. Because it was, after all, now or never, and she would never be able to summon the nerve to do this again. 'Could you just tell him, please, that Lissa says...' she took another breath '...things have changed...completely...at my end. Something very unexpected....my former commitments are, um, finished...I'm no longer... So, if he wanted....' Her voice trailed off into nervestruck incoherence.

She rang off, unable to complete the call in any rational manner. She screwed her eyes shut in mortification. Oh, God, she'd sounded like a demented halfwit. She'd wanted to come across as cool—sophisticated, even—the kind of woman who could phone up a man like Xavier Lauran and suggest an affair.

Her cheeks burned. There was no one to witness her embarrassment, but that didn't make it any easier.

Perhaps the secretary in Paris won't pass the message on— perhaps she'll just think it so stupid she'll bin it, or not even have written it down.

She hoped it were so—the very thought of Xavier being solemnly handed her incoherent stutterings was too humiliating to contemplate.

Her expression tightened. Well, it was probably for the best. It had been self-indulgence, stupid and fantastical self-indulgence, to think that she could turn the clock back. She'd had her chance with Xavier Lauran, that solitary, magical evening, and she'd had to turn it down—turn him down. Men like him didn't give second chances—and now that she'd gone and displayed herself as some kind of gibbering moron with that demented message, if he *was* given it by his secretary, the only thing he'd feel would be relief that he hadn't taken her to bed that night after all.

Forcibly, she made herself turn away and walk back to her desk. As she sat down at her PC again, a wave of flattening despair crushed down on her. Xavier Lauran would not be walking back into her life again. He had gone, and he would stay gone.

Once more the world seemed drained of colour.

After Armand's whirlwind descent, the flat seemed even more dreary than usual. And so very quiet. Even though Lissa could only rejoice at the reason, her spirits that evening were made even lower by the quiet. At least, blessedly, the evenings were her own now. That nightmare job at the casino had been the first to go after Armand's miraculous reappearance.

That was what she should focus on. Everything was wonderful now—thanks to Armand. And she had no business wanting even more.

She should never have tried to get in touch with Xavier Lauran. It had been greed, nothing more—and self-indulgence, wanting yet more good fortune on top of all that had been showered down on her.

It was not to be. She must accept that and let it go. She'd forget him soon—he was just a fantasy. A daydream. Nothing more than that.

It was easy to say, however—far less easy to heed her own advice.

She must think of Armand instead—of the miracle he had wrought, and all that was happening now in America. She longed to phone him—but she had promised to wait for news.

Please let it be good news...

He would phone her, he had promised, when there was something to tell—but until then she must be patient. He would take care of everything and take care especially of—

The piercing shrill of the doorbell shattered her thoughts in that direction.

Who on earth?

Anxiety bit at her suddenly. Surely it was not Armand? It couldn't be—it mustn't be.

The doorbell rang again. Urgent and imperative. On suddenly trembling legs she hurried to the door and unhooked the entry-phone. There was no way she was opening the front door to the street without checking first to find out who was there.

'Hello?' She made her voice sound brisk and businesslike. Not like a home alone female.

The voice at the other end was distorted, but as it penetrated her ear, faintness drummed through her.

It was Xavier Lauran.

CHAPTER EIGHT

THERE WAS SILENCE, complete silence, through the rusting grille of the entryphone system. Xavier stood, every muscle tensed.

Emotion tore at him.

Had that garbled message his PA had relayed to him with a deadpan face really been what the few incoherent words implied? The fractured phrases were burned in his mind.

Things have changed...completely...at my end. Something very unexpected... My former commitments are...finished. I'm no longer... So, if he wanted...

If the words were true it could mean only one thing.

She and Armand were finished.

It was blunt, it was brutal—but if, *if* it really were true, then—

One thought and one alone burned in his mind. *I can have her.*

Triumph surged in him. If his brother no longer had a claim on her, then those damning words of hers—*I can't*—no longer mattered. Were no longer true.

If.

So small a word, so much hanging on it.

It must be true. Why else would she have phoned?

He needed to know. Right now. Frustration stabbed at him again, poisonously mixing with hope.

Why wouldn't she open the damn door?

As if he'd spoken the words aloud, there was a sudden ping from the door and the lock yielded. He pushed it open instantly and strode inside. There was a narrow corridor, lit only by a bare bulb hanging from the ceiling. Stairs led away up from the central area. Everything looked bleak and bare. But he had eyes for none of it—only for the woman standing in the doorway of the ground-floor flat, clinging on to the doorjamb.

He went to her. He caught her to him. Dropped his mouth to hers.

His kiss was urgent, possessive, putting his brand on her. She collapsed against him, boneless. Triumph surged in him. He let her go, slipping his hands either side of her face, tilting it up to him. Her eyes were huge.

'Why did you phone me?'

His voice sounded fierce, and he saw her pupils distend even more.

'I… I…' Her voice was faint, her body still weakly collapsed against his, held upright only because of the strength in the palms of his hands, holding her face as he looked down at her, towering over her.

'I need to know,' he said, and his voice was still fierce. 'I need to know if you are free to come to me.'

There was a soft rasp in her throat. And then, as if a dam had broken inside her, she suddenly flung her arms around him and crushed her face against his shoulder. His hands slid around her back automatically, cradling her.

'Is that a yes, *cherie?*' The edge was still there, but something else, as well. His hands began to stroke up and down the length of her spine. She lifted her face away from him. Her eyes were shining like a rainbow. Something leapt in him.

Then she breathed a word—a single word.

'Xavier.' It was a sigh, it was an exhalation, it was all he needed to hear.

Very slowly, he brought his mouth down on hers again.

Exultation flowed like a rich, deep tide.

Lissa Stephens was his.

He did not mention Armand. He did not need to. There was no point. Whatever had happened between Lissa and his brother, it was over. All he knew was that he, Xavier, had done the honourable thing—he had walked away from a woman who was forbidden to him, no matter what it had cost him to do so.

And it had cost him—no doubt of that. Now, as he held her tight against him, feeling the warmth of her body in his arms, it slammed home to him just how much it had cost him, thinking that he was forever barred from her.

Relief poured through him. He could make Lissa his, and that was all he cared about. Whatever had happened between her and his brother was immaterial—it was over, and that was all that mattered. He would not think about it, would shut it out of his mind, would only tighten his arms around the woman he wanted and now had. There was only one centre of focus in his whole being—and she was in his arms. He would ask no questions, either of her or his brother. He would just accept, with relief and gratitude, that there was nothing standing between them. The tide that had started to flow so powerfully, so overwhelmingly, that moment when he had walked into the cocktail bar and seen Lissa as she truly was, could flow now unchecked until it reached the satiation it craved.

But not right here, or right now.

Reluctantly, he drew away from her glancing past her, into the interior of the wretched flat she lived in. Then his eyes came back to hers. The blast of radiance in them shook him.

'Let's go,' he said. He kissed her lightly, possessively. 'And bring your passport.'

Lissa was floating. Floating on a bubble of bliss that lifted her feet right off the ground. He had come for her. Xavier Lauran

had come for her—wanted her so much that he had flown here from Paris the moment he'd got her stuttering message.

A glow filled her, sweet and intense and radiant. As she dashed around the flat—throwing things into a small valise, hastily changing into something less frumpy than a tracksuit, turning off the hot water, unplugging electrical appliances, leaving a brief voice mail for the agency to say she was taking time off at short notice—one of the few perks of temping—gathering her purse and passport, mobile phone and anything else she knew she must take with her—she could hardly think straight.

She had gone from dejection and resignation—from forcing herself to face up to accepting that Xavier Lauran was not for her, that her chance had gone, that he was not going to come back into her life, that all she would have of him was a brief memory, a jewel kept in a secret place whose colour would slowly dim and drain away—gone from that to its complete opposite. From dejection to elation. From resignation to radiance. From monochrome to glorious colour, like a rainbow just for her.

She could feel her heart leap as she glanced up from throwing underwear helter-skelter into her valise. He filled her vision. Dear God, he just looked so breathtakingly handsome standing there, his eyes fixed on her as he leaned, with effortless elegance, against the doorjamb of the bedroom, watching her pack, watching her with that half smile of his dancing in his eyes, playing about his beautifully shaped mouth. Recalling for her the memory of the night he'd taken her to that magical dinner at his hotel.

Were they going there now? Or, if not, then where? He had said passport, so did that mean he was taking her to France—but when? For how long? She didn't care. Didn't care about anything—only that she would go with him wherever he took her.

I'm going to take this moment. Take it and relish it. I know he's only a fantasy made flesh, but for the time he wants me I will be with him and have him.

She wouldn't think about the reality of what she was doing—that was for later, not now. All she would do now was allow herself the thrill and bliss of the moment, with her feet floating off the ground, all courtesy of Xavier Lauran—here, live, freshly flown in from Paris just to claim her, waiting to take her with him.

She zipped up the valise and picked it up, along with her handbag.

'Ready?' he asked, and strolled towards her, taking her valise from her. She nodded, heart racing. It was all she could do.

'Yes,' she said.

He held out his hand to her, and she went to him.

Lissa stood in Xavier Lauran's bedroom in his apartment in Paris. It was gone midnight, and she had to pinch herself to believe that only a few hours ago she had been cleaning her drear and dingy flat in South London. Now she was in a high-ceilinged *grand appartement*, its décor a stunning mix of ancient and modern, occupying the first floor of an old courtyarded *hotel* which, a century ago, had been the town house of a wealthy Second Empire financier to Napoleon III—or so Xavier had informed her when they'd arrived. She'd been stunned to realise that Xavier intended to fly straight back to Paris that very night, whisking her right to Heathrow in the waiting car outside.

And now she was here, in Paris—with the man she had thought could never be hers.

Who was standing here, now, in front of her, a glass of champagne in his long fingers, just as she held one in hers. It was probably an exquisite vintage, she knew, but she was incapable of doing it justice. Every atom of her being was focussed on one thing, and one thing only—being here with him.

'To us, together at last,' said Xavier, and took a sip from his glass. She made herself do likewise, though she was hardly aware

of doing so. She was only aware of the man who, this very night, was going to take her to his bed.

And she would go. Willingly, ardently. Xavier Lauran wanted her—had come for her—had swept her off to Paris—and she wanted him with every cell in her body, every fibre of her being. Her breath caught for the thousandth time as she gazed up at him, at the lean, elegant body, the incredible planes of his face, and into those dark, long-lashed eyes gazing down into hers with a message in them that turned her knees to jelly, that sent her pulse soaring into the stratosphere. All thought was gone. Only the wonder and thrill of the moment possessed her.

She watched him set aside his glass on an antique tallboy, and then reach to take hers from nerveless fingers. He smiled down at her. She felt her legs dissolve. The smile was warm and intimate and for her alone. His hand lifted, and with the backs of his fingers he stroked gently down her cheek.

She could not breathe, could not speak—could only stand there while his touch caressed her. So lightly—so devastatingly. She felt her skin come alive beneath his touch, her breathing quicken suddenly as his hand turned, and now his fingertips were brushing with tantalising sensuousness over the contours of her lips.

He had stepped closer. She wasn't sure when—wasn't sure of anything except the sweet, honeying sensation that was dissolving through her.

'You are so beautiful,' he said, and his voice was soft. It sent a tremor of arousal through her, and her eyelids fluttered of their own accord as he held her eyes with his long-lashed dark gaze. She wanted to touch him. To lift her fingers to that sable hair, to feather it and run her fingertip along the high line of his cheekbone. She felt her hand lift.

He caught it. Swiftly, with a soft, encircling grip around her wrist. His hold was not hard, but she could not escape.

'No,' he told her, and his voice had the very slightest husk to it. 'First I want to touch *you*.'

She let him touch. Let the delicate pads of his fingers explore her lips, the line of her throat, the tender lobes of his ear, the sensitive nape of her neck. And then slide down, down into the valley of the blouse she had hurriedly put on. One by one he slipped the buttons, all the time his eyes holding hers, and she simply stood there, incapable of moving, incapable of anything except letting the exquisite sensation swirl slowly through her, weakening her whole body.

He parted her blouse. Already her breasts were swelling, responding to the sensuous play of his touch, and as his thumbs grazed over her nipples beneath the fine material of her bra they flowered instantly. She gave a little sigh in her throat at the sensation, and then he was sliding her blouse from her shoulders, so that it fluttered to the floor. In the same movement his fingers had slipped open the fastening of her bra, and he peeled that from her, as well.

Then his hands returned to her breasts. They were fully ripe now, heavier than they had ever been, and yet again he turned his hands over and gently, so gently, began to brush the sides of the backs over the twin orbs. The sensation was exquisite, and Lissa felt her head drop backwards, her lips parting. Yet for all the exquisiteness of the sensation there was a lack, too—a yearning within her. Her breasts lifted, and the sheer delicacy of his touch as he stroked them to yet further ripeness was almost unbearable. And then, at last, his fingers trailed over the ripened peaks, his fingers scissoring with almost leisurely enjoyment over their straining coral tips.

Sensation shot through her, quickening her, and her lips parted more.

'Xavier—' She breathed his name on an exhalation.

He didn't answer her, but the long lashes of his eyes swept down as he brought his gaze to where his fingers were.

'*Belle*—' he said softly.

For timeless moments he continued to stroke and play with her breasts, until Lissa could almost no longer bear the exquisiteness of his touch. She felt her body sway. She was hot with desire, unaware of anything except the deliciousness of the sensation in her breasts. And yet she was aware of something— aware that it was not enough, not nearly enough.

As if he read her desire for more, he slid his hands downwards, over the slender wand of her body, his fingers splaying out across her bare flanks. His hands slipped around her waist, and she felt the loosening glide of the zip of her skirt, then the swooshing fall as it cascaded to the ground. She stepped out of it, a little sideways step that she scarcely noticed. Because every atom of her being was focussed on what Xavier was doing next.

His hands were cupping the lush roundness of her bottom, fingers spread, stroking and lifting. Lifting her into himself. He let his hips rest against hers, and with a surge of sudden excitement Lissa felt the hard, revealing strength of his arousal. Her breath caught and her eyes went to his.

There was knowledge in his eyes, and a rich, deep desire.

'And now, *cherie*, it is time for you to touch me,' he said softly.

For a moment she hesitated. She was supremely conscious of the fact that she was standing against him, stripped to her skimpy panties, her breasts swollen and peaked, her hair loose down her naked back—a woman waiting to be taken to his bed while he, fully aroused, was also fully clothed. The contrast shivered through her with erotic intensity.

Her arms lifted, and she draped them loosely around his neck. The movement brought the breasts he had caressed to ripened fullness into contact with his suited body. She felt the contact of his jacket against her nipples, and the sensation excited her yet more.

Her breathing quickened yet again.

She softly pressed hips barely covered by the thin silk of her

panties against his, and felt the delicious contact there, as well. Against a yet more intimate part of her body.

She watched his face—quite deliberately. There was a line of tension along his cheekbones. It sent a thrill through her. Oh, she might be one of many women a man as gorgeous as Xavier Lauran could have for his pleasure, but right now she was the woman in his arms—she was the one who was causing that tension, that arousal, that absolute focus of his extreme attention.

It would not last. She knew it with a distant portion of her mind. But she did not care. She would pay the price when it came, and come it would, and then she would return to her real life, but for now she would have what she had never thought she would have, never thought she would experience.

For one delicious moment longer she held still, simply revelling in the feel of her silk-veiled pubis against the strength of his straining shaft, then she leaned back slightly from him, so that their hips were still in contact but she had the space to draw her hands back from around his neck.

Her fingers went to his tie. Teased open the knot. Then, never losing contact with his eyes, which were locked to hers, she slowly slid the tie out from beneath his collar. She discarded it on the floor. It lay, coiled, beside her bra and her other clothes, unseen, unattended to. She had more to attend to with her fingers.

One by one she slipped the buttons on his shirt, easing and teasing each button loose with deliberate slowness. As she worked her way down, the backs of her fingers rested on the smooth white surface of his shirt. She could feel the heat from his hard flesh beneath. Soon, so very soon, her fingers would be gliding over that smooth, firm flesh.

Opened, she eased the shirt little by little from his waistband, and then, when it was loose, her hands went back to his shoulders. His gaze was still locked to hers, still unreadable, although she knew perfectly well, with every feminine instinct, that he was

exerting supreme control over his reactions, forcing himself to stay immobile while she stripped him down to the lean, perfect body beneath the expensive tailored clothes.

Her hands, at last, slid beneath the surface of the material of his loosened shirt, and the sensation of his warm, smooth skin beneath her palms was heady in its intimacy. Her fingers cupped his shoulders and worked the shirt from his body and arms. It slithered to the floor. Only then did she allow herself the luxury of letting her hands stroke over his torso. It made her breath catch— it was perfect, quite perfect. A column of lean, muscled flesh and bone, neither over- nor under-developed, neither broad nor slim, but perfect. It was bliss to touch, bliss to let her hands roam free, drifting in slow sweeps on its surface warmth, sliding around his waist to glide up over the muscled contours of his back.

And then, most blissful of all, to lift her body against his again, and let the contact of her swollen nipples graze across his own naked, exposed flesh.

She felt his arousal strengthen, and it made her breath catch, made the excitement surge again in her. As if it were a cue for him, suddenly, from being immobile, he took control again. His hands wrapped around her back, fingers splaying out in possession.

His mouth came down on hers.

This was no soft kiss as at the hotel, nor was it urgent with relief as it was at her flat. This was the kiss of a man, a male, strong, sensual, possessing her mouth as if it was his to take for the asking. He opened her to him with effortless intent and speared within, meeting her and deepening the kiss with sensual mastery.

Desire surged in her, stronger and more insistent. She returned kiss for kiss, her hands moving up to cup the shape of his skull beneath the pressure of her fingertips, buried in the silken, sable hair.

Her body was ripe, engorged, her lips swollen, her breasts straining, and between the vee of her legs, where the strength of

his shaft pressed insistently, intimately against her, she felt a quickening that fed the hunger she must sate.

As if he felt she had reached that point, he suddenly caught her up and deposited her on the wide, soft bed. Her breath caught as he stood briefly, to strip, with controlled, swift movements, the last of his clothes. He came down beside her and in the same moment his fingers hooked into the hip-level waistline of her panties and peeled them from her. Where they fell she did not know or care. Knew only that she was lying naked to his view. And now he was perusing her, propped on one elbow, just a little way from her on the wide bed, his eyes moving over her naked body leisurely, lingeringly, until his gaze reached her eyes, and held.

It was the most intimate look he had given her yet, and Lissa knew that now they were truly about to start making love together. This was her moment of time with him.

She felt beautiful. More beautiful than she had ever felt in her life. The beauty of her naked female form, her long hair flowing out in a swathe behind her, her limbs, her body, all displayed for him, for him alone—the body of a woman in desire, a desire that she would consummate with this man, whose perfect body lay beside her, in a state of nature as was hers. There was a naturalness about it, a rightness about this coming together of two bodies, two people, giving themselves to each other.

Not in love, nor lust, but in mutual appreciation of the gift of physical sensuality.

She smiled. It was a warm smile as the recognition of the rightness of what she was doing, where she was, what was to happen, glowed in her. For just a second something veiled in his eyes—as if it might be a question, and then it was gone, banished, and he was looking down at her with an answering tug at the corner of his beautiful mouth.

'Xavier,' she said softly. A statement, a recognition. An ac-

knowledgement of what she was about to do. Make love with a man she desired above all others. 'Xavier,' she breathed again.

It was all he needed. His head lowered to hers and he began to kiss her. Slowly this time, but with such skilled, arousing sensuality that she was lost—lost in a world she had not known possible, a world where every touch, every caress, drew from her a response that intensified with every exquisite contact.

He stroked her body, his hand warm on her flanks, her breasts, smoothing and gliding over her stomach, cupping her breasts with the bowl of his hand, fingers scything slowly either side of her nipples as if the touch were as pleasurable to him as it was to her. She moved her head in the soft pillows, sensuously revelling in the sensation as his hand moved down over her flank again, dipping between the pillars of her thighs, parting them for himself.

The tips of his fingers glided between, and she was dewed for him already, her breath catching with a soft cry in her throat as the incredible sensation of pleasure and bliss focused her entire being on that portion of her body. Against her thigh, as he moved closer to her, she could feel the strong length of his bared shaft.

He moved over her. He was against her stomach now, full and hard, and his hands framed her face, his mouth lowering to hers to kiss her yet again, sensual, deep kisses.

Then he lifted his mouth from her. 'I must delay one moment,' he said, and as he raised himself from her and turned away she realised what he was doing. Her eyes fluttered shut, and she let her head tilt slightly in the opposite direction. There was the subdued slide of a drawer, another moment's delay, and then she felt his weight shift on the bed.

'You may open your eyes again, *cherie*,' he said. 'The dreadful deed is done.' There was amusement in his voice, and his hand reached to turn her head towards him again. He kissed her softly, reassuringly, and she relaxed, her eyes opening to his amused consideration. A man as experienced in affairs as Xavier Lauran

would of course, she acknowledged, be prepared to take the necessary precautions, against both disease and the threat of an unwanted pregnancy with a woman who was, after all, no more than a passing desire to him. For just a moment unease flickered within her. She had come to this point knowingly, consciously, without any seduction or persuasion, simply because she was at a moment in her life when she had the time and opportunity to seize for herself an experience she would savour, appreciate, for the rest of her life. It was not real, this fantasy of desire with Xavier Lauran, but for its duration it was sweet, and oh so potent.

And it was now—*now*. The moment of consummation, of desire fulfilled, of yearning achieved, of fantasy indulged.

He moved over her again, kissing her on her mouth, his elbows supporting the weight of his lean body, his hips against hers, his legs lying between hers, and on her abdomen rested the manhood with which he would possess her.

She was ready for him. Absolutely, completely. For this moment. Now. Her hands glided along his flanks and she felt him tense. She gazed up at him, desire in her eyes, and met his answering desire.

'Now,' she said softly. 'Now.'

He lifted away from her, his strong thighs parting hers yet a little more, and then, his fingers still cradling either side of her face, he slowly started to enter her.

She gave a long, low gasp, an exhalation of pleasure that brought the tilted smile crooking at his lips again.

'A little more?' he asked.

She only sighed in reply, not wasting breath on words to give an answer he already knew. He eased further into her, deeper. She opened to him, her silken tissues making his entrance as smooth as satin. The sensation was like nothing she had ever known, widening her, stretching her, yet entirely without pain. Only pleasure—pleasure that was more than physical sensation,

pleasure that went through her whole body, engaging every part of it, so that her blood began to throb in her veins. Her fingertips pressed into the sides of his body.

'It's so *good*,' she breathed.

He smiled at her again, and the way his mouth curved, his eyes lit, made her catch her breath again. He deepened his penetration, his hips now coming into contact with hers. Instinctively she raised her own hips, bending her knees just a little to balance herself. As she opened to him further he surged yet deeper into her, fusing her to him, and her flesh enclosed him like a lover's embrace.

She was filled—fulfilled. Entire and whole. Complete. Two bodies become as one. For precious moments he just lay like that, cradled within her, as her hands rested at his waist.

'Don't move,' she breathed. 'Just for a moment longer—don't move.'

She wanted to go on lying there, her naked body taken by his, his taken into hers, the softness of the bed cradling them. It was perfect, so perfect.

For a little while she was indulged, and she felt, if it were possible, that he seemed to grow fuller and stronger within her as her own body tightened around him in perfect unison.

Then— '*Cherie…*'

There was a thread of strain in his voice that roused her from the sweet pleasure that was so perfectly balanced between fulfilment and further desire. She gave a slow smile, and lifted her mouth to brush his lightly. Then, with the same movement, she lifted her hips fractionally.

It was all it took. He surged within her, and as he did so, his internal caress of that most sensitive place of all fused into a single, absolute point of bliss.

She gasped aloud, and he surged again, then again. Her throat arched, and his eyes locked with hers. With absolute surety of stroke he built a pyramid of bliss within her, the soft

gasping in her throat becoming almost a cry of anguish, anguish—so sweet that it was indistinguishable from the most intense pleasure.

He gave one final surge, and the incredible feeling blazed out through her body, torching it. She cried out, a sob of bliss, her eyes shutting so tightly there was nothing in the entire universe except this.

Her hands clutched him desperately, her heels digging into the bedclothes and her hips straining upwards against him to intensify the sensation that was sheeting through her. And then a new sensation impacted on her—her internal muscles were pulsing, convulsing, drawing him further, further into her, and then suddenly she felt him tense every muscle and sinew in his body, his body taut against her like an arrow in soaring flight.

He cried out, the strong muscles of his chest ridged, the cords of his throat rigid. For one timeless moment they held each other in the completion of their union, and then she could feel her body collapse in exhaustion. He closed down on her, his body warm and damp with a sheen of sweat that she realised in wonder was dewing her skin, as well. She was panting, her breath coming with unsteady inhalations against the exhausted, heavy weight of his body which she was cradling fast against her.

Wonder filled her, and an exaultation she had never known before. She felt her mouth part in a rapturous smile.

She speared her fingers into his hair—hair that was damp at the nape, tousled by her touch.

How long she lay like that, she was not sure. She was sure only that she wanted now for nothing, and that here, in this moment, was all she was and all she needed. Her eyes were closed, and she lay supine, her limbs exhausted but replete, his weight against her, his cheek against hers.

She felt him move. Softly, she felt her closed eyelids kissed.

'Ma belle,' he said.

Then he started to withdraw his weight—and more than his weight.

'Do not move. I will be but a moment,' he assured her.

Yet even that brief time apart from him left her feeling cold, abandoned, so that when he returned to her she held out her arms to him, wrapped him to her and clung to him.

'Xavier,' she breathed into his skin, inhaling the scent of him. Then, as her eyelids closed again, she felt drowsiness sweep over her.

Dimly, she felt the covers being drawn over her. Dimly she heard him murmur something. Dimly she registered that the lights had been extinguished, and then, still cradled against him, held in the strong circle of his arms, she went to sleep.

For a while longer Xavier lay, looking up into the darkness overhead. What had happened? He had known he had wanted Lissa—that her beauty had struck him like a *coup de foudre* that night at the hotel, overpowering all his logic and reason and sense, stimulating in him a desire that had swept him away. He had been known that his thwarted desire for her had been a torment, and that he had continued to want her with an intensity that had been sharpened to unbearableness by the knowledge that she was beyond his reach, reserved for Armand, his own brother. And he had known, ever since that out-of-the-blue message had sent him chasing from Paris to London to claim her, that possessing her finally, as he now had, would be a release and a satiation all the sweeter because he had not thought to have it.

But what had just happened had gone beyond that.

Why? How?

He asked the questions, but his rational mind could find no answer. No reason. He was in unknown territory, that was all he knew. A place he had not been before. He tried to put it into

words. As his mind searched, as he stared up into the darkness, he could feel the soft warmth of her body curled against him.

The reality of her presence in his arms, his bed, swept over him. What did anything matter compared with that? It was all that was important—all he would allow himself.

He shifted his limbs to ease them a moment. As he did, the weight of her soft, warm body shifted, too, bearing down on him more. He heard her murmur in her sleep, her dream. She lay so peacefully in his arms. So naturally.

She felt good to hold. Good to lie with.

Good to fall asleep beside.

He felt his focus dissolve, the drowsiness of post-coital satiation wash up over him. His eyes started to feel heavy and close, his breathing slowed. Instinctively for one second his arms tightened around her, checking she was still there. He let his body relax, his mind, too.

He slept in her embrace, embracing her.

It felt very good.

CHAPTER NINE

SUNLIGHT, AND THE smell of fresh, fragrant coffee stirred the senses of Lissa's sleeping mind, luring her to wakefulness. As she surfaced from slumber she wondered why she felt so wonderful—and then she remembered. Her eyes flew open.

She was alone in the bed, but Xavier was sitting on the edge, clad only in a short white bathrobe that accentuated the fabulous golden tan of his skin and exposed—she gave a silent gulp—the smooth muscled surface of his chest and forearms. Her eyes flew to his and clung.

He leaned forward and kissed her softly on the mouth.

'Bonjour, *cherie*.' He smiled.

She felt her heart melt into a puddle inside her. Her eyes lit.

'Xavier.'

A huge, joyous smile broke across her face.

It had been true, not a dream. A wonderful, blissful truth that made her breathless with delight. Xavier had swept down on her and scooped her up and borne her away to Paris, the most romantic of cities, to make her his. Her smile deepened and her eyes drank in the beautiful planed face of the man looking down at her, amusement and bemusement glittering in his eyes in equal measures.

Long, silky lashes swept down over his eyes.

'Would you like coffee?' he asked.

The aromatic, heady fragrance tickled at her nose again. 'Oh— Please,' she answered.

She started to sit up and then remembered, with a little thrill, that she wasn't wearing a stitch. Sudden confusion and embarrassment swept over her, and she clutched the rumpled duvet to her breasts as she sat herself up. Xavier leaned around her and propped up the pillow. The silk of his hair brushed against her jaw as he did so, and her heart melted again. As he straightened and she leaned back against the head of the bed, she pushed back her own tumbled hair with fingers that trembled suddenly.

'Black or white?'

His hand hovered over a jug of hot milk that stood on the coffee tray on the bedside table.

'Oh— White, please—thank you.'

Her voice sounded breathless, even to her, and suddenly she was too shy to look him in the eye. She took the *grande tasse* and raised it to her lips for a tiny sip of hot, pale coffee, glad he had busied himself pouring his own cup and then settling back, one leg crooked under him on the wide bed, to drink it. As he did so she stole a look at him, feeling that thrill go through her again.

Her face opened into a huge, joyous smile of delight and wonder.

'Did it really happen?'

The words came from her before she could stop them. Dark eyes lifted and looked into hers.

'I thought it might all have been a dream,' she said haltingly, her eyes meeting his, only to drown in their depths. 'It was just so wonderful!'

A smile played at the corner of his sculpted mouth, and again there was that mixed look of amusement and bemusement in his dark eyes.

'It was my pleasure,' he murmured. his French accent making her insides quiver.

'Mine, too,' she blurted. 'Heaps and heaps—' She cut off dead,

and, biting her lip, made a face. 'I'm sorry, I'm being— What's the French term? *Jejeune?* Is that it? Or—' she made another face '—maybe just *naïf.* Anyway.' She swallowed, 'Um, er— Well.' Hastily she drank some more coffee, dropping her head so that her tumbled hair covered her embarrassment at behaving like an idiot.

Fingers gently touched the side of her head.

'Look at me,' Xavier said.

She made herself do so. He leaned forward and kissed her on her forehead. And suddenly it was all right, just fine, and not embarrassing at all, and she gave a wide smile again. Happiness filled her like a warm balloon, and she felt that familiar feeling of starting to float up from the ground.

She met his eyes, and now it was all right—more than all right. It was fine and lovely and—right. That was the word for it. Not that she wanted to think about words just at the moment—or about anything, really. She just wanted to go on feeling as if she was lighter than air, and happy and floating. Sunlight filled the room—bright sunlight from drawn-back curtains—sending golden dust motes shimmering through the air.

'Everything is good, *cherie,*' he told her softly, 'because you are here with me.' He lowered his mouth to brush hers lightly, lingeringly. Then he drew back, nodding towards the coffee she still held.

'Drink up,' said Xavier, that half smile at his mouth again. It made his mouth even more beautiful, thought Lissa dreamily.

Obediently, she took another mouthful of coffee, the fragrance and taste of it carrying with it all that was France—pavement cafés and sunlit balconies. She watched Xavier drink from his own cup, and everything about the gesture registered as if in ultra-focus—the way his hand was splayed under the saucer, holding the weight of the cup, the elegant turn of his wrist as he lifted the cup, the fall of his hair as he lowered his head slightly to drink. Dreamily, she took another draught.

Then, '*Ça suffit.*' It was decisively spoken, and then Xavier was setting down his cup, and removing hers from her grasp. For a moment, just a moment, Lissa's eyes widened in alarm and anxiety. Was he going to send her packing now? Politely, of course, and charmingly, but packing all the same. Put her on a plane back to London, and get on with his own life.

But as he straightened and turned back to her she realised, with a dissolving stomach, that sending her packing was the last thing on his mind. That decisiveness had not been about getting on with his busy day, but about—

His kiss was long and slow and warm, and dissolved not only her stomach but every cell in her body. She gave herself to it, to the soft, sensuous delight of it. Her hands slid of their own volition across the smooth wall of his half-bared chest, her body sliding down into the bed. His mouth caressed hers, and she gave herself, wholly and entirely, to the soft, sensuous delight that was Xavier Lauran making the most beautiful love in the world to her.

They stayed one day in Paris.

'I must clear my desk, *hélas,*' he told her ruefully. 'But tomorrow morning we can leave.'

'Where are we going?' she asked, wide-eyed.

'You'll see,' he answered, a half smile playing on his face.

He knew exactly where he was going to spend this time with her. The season was a little early, but it was better than the heat of summer, and there would be no crowds to get in their way. It was a place he never took his *amours* to, but Lissa was different. Different how, exactly, he still did not ask—or answer. He only knew that the kind of *affaire* he was used to would not work with her. Lissa was not someone to leave in his apartment while he kept up his daily routine of business meetings and high-pressure work, spending only evenings with her in restaurants, or at the theatre

or the opera, or social engagements, as had been his custom with
Madeline and her predecessors over the years. No, he wanted
Lissa to himself twenty-four-seven—safe by his side, in his bed.
He had thought her forever forbidden to him—and now that fate
had given her to him after all he would not neglect her.

So it was well worth breaking his neck all day, driving his PA
and directors as if the devil were chasing them, in his attempt to
clear his desk of all essential tasks. Some were impossible to
complete, and those he could not postpone he undertook to do
remotely. A couple of hours a day on the laptop, in communication with his office, would be the maximum he would commit to.

Besides, he argued to himself, when had he last taken a
holiday? He gave an ironic grimace—the French took more
holidays than most other nationalities, and his staff, like all
sensible people, made the most of them, but he, running the
whole company, seldom took time off.

Well, now he would. Now, with the woman he had thought
never to have beside him, he would for once play hooky.

Even as he formed the thought, another plucked at his mind.

What about Armand? Should he not contact him? Find out
how it was that he and Lissa had parted?

He blocked it out. It didn't matter what had happened between
them—all that mattered was that Lissa was not bound to his
brother anymore, and was free to come away with him instead.
After all, hadn't Armand asked him not to interfere in his affairs
of the heart? And hadn't he learned—almost at a cost that chilled
him to contemplate—that it would have been wiser by far to have
done just that? Instead he had blundered in, intent on doing his
best for his brother, guarding him from making a mistake that
would cost him dear. No, this time around he would do nothing.
Armand's life was his own—whatever had happened between
him and Lissa was not his concern. All that *was* his concern was
that the woman he had so catastrophically desired when she was

his brother's intended wife had now, wonderfully, been set free for him to claim.

Had Lissa been in love with Armand? No, that was impossible. There was not the slightest vestige of a broken heart, or any such thing. If he had not known what Armand had been to her, he might never have guessed at the recent presence in her life of any other man.

For a brief moment a flicker of, not unease, but perhaps uncertainty glimmered in his mind. He blocked it out. Appearances had been deceptive when it came to Lissa—none knew that better than he. His first sight of her had made him think her a cheap *putain*. How wrong he had been. It had been a mask, that cheap, tacky appearance—a costume necessary for her job. And though he naturally would have preferred that she had never worked at the casino, that was all over now anyway. Besides, she had been prepared to lose her job rather than compromise herself morally. So that, again, was another mark in her favour.

And she had turned him down because of her commitment to Armand.

That was what had convinced him about her. She had resisted him because of her brother.

Memory flickered in his mind again.

Someone very important to me…

That was how Lissa had described Armand to him—not knowing that she was talking about his own brother.

Was Armand still important to her?

No—he could not be. Certainly not emotionally—he had established that already, and her very presence in his bed confirmed it. Financially, then? Perhaps—he had to consider the possibility. Seeing inside the grim place she lived had brought home even more forcibly just how impoverished her life was. He could understand Armand, with his wealth and social position, being a temptation to her. And while—as was obvious—she had

not loved Armand as a wife should love her husband, still that did not mean she had not held him in regard. Certainly enough to turn down another man. Even when she had responded to his desire for her she had still said no.

Besides, Armand's e-mail had said he hadn't yet proposed to her. She might not even have realised he was in love with her, wanted to marry her—yet she had still turned him down that night because of Armand's presence in her life.

Whatever had changed Armand's mind about her—or even hers about him—there was only one thing of importance now. Whatever Armand might have wanted—might still want—it was too late.

She is with me—that is all I care about. She is free to come to me. I have claimed her, and she is mine.

He would think no more than that.

'Xavier, no! I can't accept—I really can't.'

For answer he waved an impatient hand. 'I insist,' he said.

Her mouth looked mutinous for a moment. 'I won't let you buy me clothes.'

Xavier took her hands in the middle of the formidably chic *salon* of one of the top French couture houses, where he had taken her after breakfast the morning they were due to leave Paris.

'Do it for me, *cherie*. To keep me happy. I want to see your beauty set off to perfection.'

She bit her lip. 'I can't,' she said. 'It isn't right.'

He gave a Gallic shrug. 'Then why not regard them as a loan—nothing more—as you did the dress at the hotel?'

She frowned a moment. 'What did you do with it, anyway? That dress?'

He shrugged again. 'I believe I gave it to the maid. She was very grateful.'

Lissa's eyes widened. 'That was very generous—it cost a fortune. But not—' she grimaced, looking about her in this

bastion of high fashion '—as much as anything here will cost.'
She looked at him straight. 'Xavier, it's not just that I can't accept
you buying clothes for me, but it's because I don't want you
spending your salary like this. I'm not sure how senior you are
at XeL, but even so—'

There was the very slightest cough from the stick-thin, scarily
chic *vendeuse,* hovering at a discreet distance. At least, it might
have been a cough, or possibly more like a smothered choke. It
certainly drew a forbidding glance from Xavier. Then he looked
back at Lissa.

'Let's just say I buy clothes here at cost.' He paused minutely.
'XeL has a cross-holding with this particular design house which
allows that. I get a discount.'

Lissa looked at him suspiciously. 'How much of a discount?'

'A substantial one,' he answered smoothly.

It seemed to do the trick, and she gave in, contenting herself
with merely stipulating that she would let him buy her—*loan
her*—no more than three garments. As she selected them and
went to try them on Xavier pondered whether to tell her that not
only was XeL a co-owner of this couturier, but that his salary was
that of chief executive and majority shareholder.

He decided against it. She had shown little interest in his work,
or XeL—her initial description of XeL as a posh luggage company
still rankled slightly—and so far as he was concerned that was all
to the good. But he still wanted to see her in decent clothes.

Even though they would be for his eyes only. Where he was
taking her would not be in the public eye.

Was it deliberate? Keeping her away from the world he moved
in? It could well be, he acknowledged. Was it the last streak of
caution or suspicion in his ultra-rational French soul? Not letting
her see just how glittering his lifestyle could be? Or was it that he
wanted her attention exclusively on himself—and his on her?
That was more plausible.

Or was it even, he mused, that Lissa Stephens did not seem
to be a woman impressed by displays of wealth? She really had
seemed averse to his buying that dress for her in London, and
now her objections here, where he'd actually had to trot out
some rigmarole about getting a discount—clearly to the amusement of the *vendeuse,* who knew exactly who he was, of course,
and had all but choked when Lissa had worried about whether
he could afford such largesse.

Speaking of which…

A few short instructions to the *vendeuse* sorted the matter.
Lissa might think she was only setting out with three paltry
outfits, but Xavier had other plans. Now that the *vendeuse* had
her measurements, she could easily provide the rest of her
wardrobe. True, where they was going she would not require a
large range of formal attire, but she would still need a lot more
than the three outfits she was letting him buy. Satisfied, he then
dedicated his attention to viewing the first outfit Lissa had
emerged to model for him.

Half an hour later everything was complete. Lissa was wearing not the chainstore skirt and blouse she had arrived in, but an
impeccably cut dress and jacket that finally did justice to her
beauty.

Tucking Lissa's hand proprietarily into his arm, leaving the
salon staff to load the boot of his car waiting outside, he made
his exit. The airport was their next stop, and then Nice. But not
to the fleshpots of the Côte d'Azur. To somewhere far more
private—where he and Lissa could be quite alone together.

Xavier lounged back in a padded chair on the small stone terrace,
and let himself be diverted from the market report he was skimming through more out of a sense of duty than any real interest.
Though he had, perforce, brought work with him, it was not
holding his attention.

But then, nothing during the last two weeks had held his attention—except Lissa.

She fitted in perfectly here. What doubts he might have had had been dispelled the moment he'd helped her into the launch waiting for them at the marina after their flight from Paris had landed at Nice.

'Where are we going?' she'd asked, eyes wide.

'I have a villa,' he'd told her. 'But it is not on the mainland. Have you heard of the Îles de Lérins?'

She'd shaken her head.

'They are a short distance from the coast, near Cannes. In the high season the two main ones, the Île St Honorat and the Île Ste Marguerite, are popular for daytrippers, but this early in the year less so. Besides, my villa is on the smallest of the islands, Île Ste Marie—barely more than an islet.' He'd smiled down into her eyes. 'I hope you will like it.'

She had loved it.

As she had exclaimed with pleasure at the simple stone-built villa, hidden beneath fragrant pine trees on a secluded promontory of the tiny island, facing the setting sun, Xavier had felt a last knot inside him dissolve. He had bought this place on impulse, several years ago. He already owned an apartment in Monte Carlo, but that was for entertaining only—for occasions when he had to be on show as the head of XeL, at fashionable events such as the Monaco Grand Prix. This small villa could not have been more of a contrast from the modern, opulent duplex in Monte Carlo, with its panoramic views over the harbour. Though he seldom had time to come here, whenever he did he always wished he could stay longer. Though only ten minutes by fast launch from the mainland, it was a world away on these unspoilt, rural islands.

He did not bring his *amours* here.

For a moment he tried to imagine Madeline de Cerasse here,

or any of the similar women he'd had affairs with, and failed completely. They would have been completely out of place, pestering him to take them back to his Monte Carlo apartment, disliking being stuck here, away from the fashionable restaurants and nightspots where they could socialise and dress up to the nines.

But Lissa—

He lifted his head from the tedium of market analysis by sector and geographical location, and let his eyes rest with pleasure on her. She was clambering over the rocks of the little cove the villa overlooked, as lithe as a gazelle, and with her hair caught up in a ponytail and wearing shorts and a T-shirt, as youthful looking as a schoolgirl.

He watched her gain the land again and set off towards him.

Xavier's eyes fixed on her. Even in such simple clothes she looked breathtaking, young, fit and natural.

That word again. It came to him over and over again whenever he looked at her or thought about her. She put nothing on for him—no arts, no lures, no *coquetterie*. She took enjoyment in what he offered her, and…enjoyed it. Enjoyed him. Enjoyed everything of their time together.

As did he her.

Had he ever been this relaxed with a woman? Or this content—just to sit watching her, being with her?

It was a strange thought, and not one that he had had before.

She came up to him, perching herself on a corner of the table that stood on the terrace, at which they generally ate breakfast and lunch. As it always did when she set eyes on Xavier, Lissa's heart squeezed. She had thought him devastating in business clothes—or none at all, she blushed mentally—but in casual clothes such as the chinos he was wearing now, with a polo shirt stretched across his lean torso, his hair slightly ruffled, he looked even more devastating, lounging back on the padded chair with a lithe grace that made her breath catch.

Was she really, truly here with Xavier? Or was it some fantasy she was imagining real? Yet the glow of her body as she looked at him told her that it was real. Every day—and every night. Real and rapturous.

And it was a rapture that just seemed to get more and more blissful. Every time, it seemed to her, dazed and amazed, was better than the last. In Xavier's arms she had discovered a sensuality that she had never known she possessed. Although he was clearly so very much more skilled in the exquisite art of love-making than she was, she never felt inadequate or inexperienced—never felt that she could not give the same pleasure as he gave her in such breathtaking abundance. And that, she recognised, was the greatest skill of all—to make her feel that she was as beautiful, as sensual, as desirable as she knew he would want a woman to be. She glowed in his arms, and came alive in a way she had never known before.

And it was not just when she was in his arms that he made her feel beautiful and desirable. With every look, she read it in his eyes. And it sent a thrill through her that she treasured.

And a glow that warmed her. Warmed her deep into the core of her being. Just being here, with him. With Xavier.

Yet it troubled her, that warmth she felt. Into her head, words darted a warning: *be careful.*

She did not—would not—put into words or even thoughts what it was she was warning herself about, but she knew, with some inner instinctive sense of danger, that she must heed that warning.

The blind fate that had taken so much from her in a handful of moments on that terrible day of twisted metal had all but destroyed everything she had once thought would be there for ever. In the same unfathomable way, it had given her this radiantly happy time now. Xavier Lauran had walked into her life—she knew not why, only that fate had made it happen, had given her this gift. For that was what he was to her, she knew. A gift.

Coming from nowhere and, she knew, with clear, non-decieving eyes, going to nowhere.

There was no future with Xavier. There could not be. He was like a glass of the finest vintage champagne, handed to her by the whim of that same fate that had taken so much from her. She would drink the champagne that was her time with Xavier to the full. She would let him go to her head like champagne.

But she would be wise, and never let him go to her heart.

And now, with the bubbles beading at the brim, she gazed smilingly across at him from her perch on the table. She was at ease with him—had been at ease for all their time together. What had they done, day after day? Their nights had been spent in each other's arms, full of passion and desire that melted the bones in her body, that took her to ecstasy and beyond. Their days had been spent easily, drifting, slipping away one by one. The deep exhaustion that had been a constant part of her life for so long had finally drained out of her in the lazy, lotus-eating days they'd passed here. There was no work to be done in the little villa—a local couple took care of housekeeping and meals and what little gardening there was to attend to on the private grounds.

What did they do each day? She tried to think. They breakfasted late—for sleep came late after lovemaking, and had a tendency to be interrupted by yet more in the night, and their *levée* was languorous and sensual and protracted. They lingered over breakfast, feasting on fragrant coffee and fresh croissants, with the aroma mingling with the tangy scent of the pine trees and the sun shafting between their trunks, glittering on the azure sea beyond. They would read, and sun themselves, and take a walk through the pine woods or along the sea's edge. Though it was too cold to swim, the shoreline was beautiful and deserted. There was a motorboat drawn up in the cove, a little one, with an outboard motor, and Xavier had taken her out in it, pottering around the islands, crossing over to the larger, more populated

ones. She had loved the Île St Honorat, with its working monastery and old medieval fortifications, and even the twin Île of Ste Marguerite, though its natural beauty had been dimmed by the sad tale of the Man in the Iron Mask, who had been so mysteriously incarcerated in the now-ruined fortress there in the seventeenth century. But both islands had been peaceful and beautiful, with wooded walks and secret beaches.

Xavier had offered to take her to the mainland once, but she hadn't wanted to go. Her reluctance was not only because she could see little appeal in the overdeveloped coastline, with its marinas stuffed with massive yachts, and its shoreline built up with hotels and high-rise apartments. There was another reason, too—and it was not just because she revelled in having Xavier to herself.

It was because here, on this tiny, secluded isle, she could keep the outside world at bay. Here, she was utterly with Xavier, thinking only of Xavier, being only with Xavier. Absorbing all her mind, her time.

Keeping her mind very far away from what was happening in America, and when she would hear again from Armand.

She did not want to think about that. Did not want that biting undercurrent of anxiety to well up when there was nothing she could do about it. All she could do was wait until Armand contacted her. Then she would know.

Until then, she had Xavier. And she must make the most, the *very* most of him. How short a time she had with him.

Anguish pierced at her, but she pushed it aside. She would not let it spoil this brief, precious time. This magical, wonderful time. All that she would have with him.

Now, reaching out one bare leg, she toed the market report that Xavier held in his hands. She grinned across at him.

'Oh, chuck the boring old report, Xavier, and come beach-combing with me,' she teased.

'Beachcombing?' he echoed, with a humorous frown at the colloquialism.

'You know—wandering along the beach to see what you can find.'

'But there is no beach, only rocks,' he objected.

She made a face. 'Oh, you French are so logical. Do come. The water may be freezing, but it's absolutely beautiful and crystal-clear.' She looked about her and took a deep breath. 'I love the scent of the pines—it permeates everything.'

He gave a smile, putting down the report, glad to do so. 'You have missed the mimosa, which is a shame—its scent is quite exquisite. We're missing the lavender, too—we saw the fields on the Île St Honorat, remember, where the monks grow it to make their liqueur.' He cocked an eyebrow at her. 'Would you like to visit Grasse while we are here? It is the centre of the perfume industry in France—and XeL has a *parfumerie* there which I could show you. And we really should go to St Paul de Vence, which is not too far from there. The Matisse chapel is nearby, and in the village itself is the celebrated Colombe d'Or Hotel, which has its very own art collection from the famous artists who stayed there. We should have lunch there.' He made a rueful face. 'I have shown you very little of the Cote d'Azur, *hélas*.'

He sounded regretful as he watched Lissa drop with her innate grace into the lounger beside him.

'It hasn't bothered me,' she assured him. 'I'm happy here at the villa. Blissfully so!'

It was true she could hardly recall ever knowing such happiness, as she had here in their private, secret world, with their private, secret happiness.

She sought to rationalise her reluctance to leave the island and the villa.

"I wish the whole Riviera were still like this—just pine trees

and a rocky shoreline, with a few villas and *maquis* up in the hills, with deserted bays and headlands and beaches every few miles. It's such a shame it's been so spoilt.' She caught herself as she finished, and it was her turn to put on a rueful expression. 'I'm sorry—I should not be so critical.'

But he was not offended—far from it. 'There are still some parts that are not concreted over,' he said with a half smile. 'Up in the hills, away from the coast in the Alpes Maritimes, where St Paul de Vence is, for example, is far less spoilt. Even on the coast there are some parts less ugly and less modern. Beaulieu, between Nice and Monte Carlo, still lives up to its name of "beautiful place" and just on the Italian border Menton could still be mistaken for the last century, or even the one before. My mother lives there with my stepfather—'

He broke off suddenly. Then, scarcely missing a beat, he resumed.

'Antibes, too, is far less touristy—a working town—and on the Cap d'Antibes is the Musée de Napoleon. Did you know that he landed on the coast there when he escaped from Elba?'

Lissa was diverted, as Xavier had intended. It had been a slip of the tongue to mention his mother and stepfather.

'Didn't the King send an iron cage for him to be imprisoned in when he was captured?' she said, groping in her memory.

Xavier laughed. 'That was what Marshal Ney promised to do. He'd turned from Bonapartist to Bourbonist after the Restoration. He set off with an army to stop Napoleon in his tracks—iron cage and all. But instead he went over to him, and his army, too. Then Napoleon marched on Paris.'

'To meet his Waterloo,' Lissa finished. 'Trounced by the English!'

Xavier shook his head and gave a laugh. 'Ah, your Wellington only beat him thanks to the Prussians. Napoleon had won the battle already, but the Prussian army arrived in the nick of time

to save Wellington's neck. Don't they teach you proper history in English schools?'

His eyes were dancing, and Lissa grinned. 'We're just taught that we won, that's all,' she said impishly. She tugged at his arm. 'Anyway, you're only trying to talk about history to get out of coming down to the beach with me. Come on, lazybones! We need some exercise before lunch.'

Xavier caught her fingers and started to nibble one.

'I can think of excellent exercise—and we don't even have to walk ten metres,' he murmured, with a glint in his eyes.

But Lissa got to her feet and tugged at him again. With a show of reluctance he stood up, tossing the market report aside on the table.

'*Eh, bien*—let us go and comb the beach, then, if you insist,' he said resignedly. Long lashes swept down over his eyes as he baited her gently.

He took her hand and she felt its warmth and strength closing around her fingers, making her feel suddenly safe and cherished.

A little tremor went through her, and, like a ghost whispering in her head, she heard again the warning to be careful.

She heard the words, felt them imprinting, but in their wake came another whisper, that set through her a deeper tremor yet.

Too late.

'Honestly, Xavier, you're such a wimp. The water's not *that* cold.'

Lissa grinned with amused exasperation at Xavier's adamant refusal to do as she was. They'd gained the headland of the tiny promontory, scrambling over rocks to get there, and were now sitting on a large, flat rock that projected slightly over the sea. Lissa had not hesitated to take off her canvas shoes and dangle her toes in the water. It was cold, no doubt about it, but that was hardly adequate reason for wimping out.

Xavier was sitting beside her, his legs drawn up, arms

loosely looped around his splayed knees. He cast her a disdainful look.

'Masochism has never appealed to me, *cherie*,' he informed her. 'And don't even dream of thinking that I'm going to rub the circulation back into your feet when they get frostbite.'

She laughed, leaning back on her elbows, letting her hair pool on the sun-warmed rock, and gazed up at him.

'You've obviously never been to the British seaside, then, have you?' she teased. 'Let alone St Andrew's up in Scotland. That's what I call cold water—even in summer! It's a fantastic beach, though, even if it is the North Sea. It's right by the famous golf course, and my father loved to play there—'

She broke off. There was a painful lump in her throat suddenly.

Xavier's attention shifted from contemplating the way her posture so invitingly thrust up her breasts. It was rare to hear Lissa mention her family. Actually, now that he thought about it, she never did. Neither did he—for obvious reasons—apart from that slip of the tongue he'd made about his mother living in Menton.

Where was her family? he wondered. Then, deliberately, he put the question from him. He didn't want to think about families—hers or his. Didn't want to think about her existence anywhere but here. Didn't want to remember the job she'd done, or how she'd been involved with his brother. He wanted to shut all that out of his consciousness. He only wanted her to be here, with him, alone at his villa, secluded from the world beyond, in a private haven where he could have her all to himself, without the interference and complications of the outside world.

Yet, unwanted thoughts flickered at him. He might want to, but he could not remain here indefinitely. Already, the two weeks he'd allowed himself from the office had overrun. How much longer could he put off returning to Paris? He was already receiving agitated e-mails from his PA and directors, indicating that they needed his full attention focussed on XeL again.

Irritation and annoyance shafted through him. He didn't want to think about XeL. He didn't want to have to go back to Paris, make decisions, take meetings, involve himself with his job again. Not yet, anyway.

This time was too precious to him.

He gazed down at Lissa. She had shut her eyes, relaxed back on her elbows, face lifted to the sun.

He felt emotion dart through him. It was desire, he knew. Familiar and enjoyable. He let his eyes roam over the exquisite lines of her face. It gave him pleasure every time he did so. He could look at her for ages.

There was something serene in her face now, lifted to the sun, hair falling back from her head. Her long, delicate lashes brushed against her cheek, flushed with the beginning of a pale tan. The gentle breeze coming off the water played with the strands of her hair, caressing her skin.

His breath caught suddenly.

Elle est si belle!

More than beautiful.

More than desirable.

Something moved in him—something he did not recognise but could feel, like a strange, alien presence.

What was it? He tried to think, to understand with his mind. His reason. But he could not. Words formed in her mind. Words he could not stop.

I don't want to let her go.

That strange, alien emotion moved through him again, and he felt its presence, stronger now. He could give it no name.

But one thing he could give a name to. One thing he knew and understood with absolute certainty. As he gazed down into her unseeing face, tracing with his eyes the line of her features, the outline of her tender, generous mouth, he knew there was only one thing to be done here, on this secluded rock, beneath the warm sun.

He let his lips move down over hers, easing them apart with a languorous sensuality. A hand curved, as if on its own, around the soft swell of her breast.

He felt her response, felt her mouth begin to move against his, and with a deep, abiding sense of satisfaction and enjoyment he began to make love to her, slowly, exquisitely, beneath the sun.

CHAPTER TEN

AFTER DINNER, AS they sat over coffee, candles burning low on the rough-hewn table in the single living room of the villa, the embers of a fire dying away to keep the faint night chill at bay, Xavier told Lissa he had to return to Paris the day after next.

'I can avoid it no longer,' he said, his voice flat. 'I'm sorry.'

A stone congealed in Lissa's insides. Hard and horrible. She made herself speak.

'Of course. I understand. It was good that you could take this time off.' Her words were jerky.

'It's a damnable nuisance,' Xavier said with sudden emphasis.

She gave a tight smile. 'It's your job. I understand that. Work doesn't give us choices.' Had her voice sharpened as she'd said that last bit? She didn't know. Didn't care. Only knew that all of a sudden the idyll was over.

Just like that.

She'd known it must happen—known with her brain, her reason. But not with anything else. With the rest of her she had only known that here, on this island, so close to the mainland and yet a million miles away from anywhere, she wanted that time with Xavier to go on for ever.

But of course it would end. Must end. She knew that—and as for him, however senior he was at XeL, he had work to do, re-

sponsibilities to meet. If anything, the more senior the executives were, the longer hours they worked. If his boss was now cracking the whip, wanting him back at his desk, then obviously he'd have to go. That was all there was to it. No one knew better than she the harsh obligation of work…

And so it was all over.

Over.

The word tolled in her mind. The stone inside her seemed heavier, choking her.

Over. All over.

Xavier would go back to Paris. She would be put back on a plane to London. He would kiss her goodbye, tell her that it had been a wonderful holiday, smile down at her—and walk away.

She would never see him again.

Pain—sudden, piercing, unbearable—sliced into her. Oh, God, how could she bear it? Never to see him again—for all this to be over?

The end of the affair.

The blunt, bleak words burned in front of her retinas. The end of the affair.

That was all it was—an affair. All it could ever be.

She had gone into it walking on air, knowing only that a fantasy had come to life, that she was being given a gift, a wonderful gift, that she had not expected. She had received it and been enraptured by it. And now it was over. All over.

Xavier was speaking again. She forced herself to listen. The stone inside her seemed to be swelling, taking her over, blocking out everything else that existed. What was he saying? She stared at him, trying to listen.

'…Paris, probably for about a week. Then I have to fly to Vienna, possibly via Munich, and later in the month I'll probably have to go to the Far East. XeL has factories there, and we keep a close eye on them to ensure working conditions are good for

the employees. I know it means a lot of travelling for you, but I'll try and ensure we get some time for sightseeing, and we would be together, which is the main thing, so—' He broke off. 'Lissa? What is it?'

She was staring at him, somewhat confusedly.

'You want—?' She swallowed. The stone was in her throat now, but something was happening to it as she made herself speak. 'You want me to come with you?'

It was his turn to stare. Then, slowly, he nodded.

'You seem surprised.' His expression changed. Across the table, he held out a hand to her. 'Did you think this was all I wanted?' His voice had softened, his eyes melted chocolate.

Slowly, numbly, she placed her hand in his. The warmth of his fingers enclosed hers. Safe. Cherishing.

And into her head the warning formed once more—*be careful*.

But they were words, only words. What power had they against the warm clasp of his hand? What power against the expression in his eyes, holding hers? What power against the surge of emotion thrilling through her as she took in what he had just said to her?

None.

Yet she had to listen.

Anguish pierced her. She said nothing. Dared say nothing. Dared show nothing. Instead, all she could do was feel the strength of his grasp on her hand, feel the warmth flowing through her, meeting the chill that was forming inside her.

Anguish pierced again.

Xavier wanted her. Wanted her for more than what he had already given her. How much more she did not know—only that he was telling her the fantasy was not yet over.

If only—

Her heart clenched. How could she? How could she fly away with Xavier? This time she'd had was time stolen from the reality of her life—she had always known that. Armand's magic wand

had lifted from her all the burdens that had crushed her, allowing her this wonderful, rapturous piece of time with Xavier.

But Armand would return.

Would he bring the news she so desperately longed to hear? She couldn't know. She could only wait.

Never had it seemed so hard, her promise not to phone him. To wait, as she had promised him.

Emotion edged like a knife blade, cutting her in half. Tearing her in two.

She slipped her hand from Xavier's.

'I didn't know,' she said, in a low, troubled voice. 'I didn't know you wanted more than what we have had here.'

He gave a curious smile, half mocking of himself.

'No more did I, *cherie*. But now—' his voice changed '—I do know.' He reached for his coffee and took a draught. 'I *do* know.' There was decision in his voice. Resolution.

The stone formed again in Lissa's chest. A line of some ancient verse stabbed in her mind: *If the gods wish to torment you, they grant you your dearest wish.*

She could say nothing. What was there to say? Nothing. Not yet, at any rate. Not now. She would not spoil this precious remaining time. Would keep it safe to the last moment.

She lifted her eyes to Xavier. She could not have him long— but while she did she would take from this time everything she could. Emotion blazed in her eyes suddenly, and for one heady moment she met his. Something dissolved inside her.

'Thank you,' she said in a low, intense voice. 'Thank you for asking me to come with you.'

She could say no more, only gaze at him, her eyes expressive of everything she felt. His coffee cup clicked as he set it back on the table with a sharp movement. With an equally abrupt movement he got to his feet. He held out his hand to her again. Imperative—demanding.

Inviting.

'Come,' he said. It was all he had to say.

She got to her feet, her pulse surging, and let him take her where he wanted to take her—where she would always want to go. The place she longed above all to be. In his arms.

Lissa turned off the shower and wrapped herself in a voluminous bath towel. Her thoughts were troubled. Emotions criss-crossed through her, powerful and disturbing.

Xavier wanted her—desired her. She knew that. Knew it every time he took her in his arms. And he had said he wanted to take her with him when they left the island.

But how can I? How can I until I know...until Armand phones me...?

Surely he must phone soon?

I have to know—I have to!

She padded out of the bathroom, her bare feet on the cool tiles, into the bedroom. It was early still. Xavier was still asleep, and of their own volition Lissa's feet took her to stand beside him. She gazed down. Emotions swirled around inside her, taunting her. Strong and overpowering. Conflicting and confusing.

She almost reached down to touch a stray lock of hair on his forehead as he lay relaxed in sleep, his long dark lashes brushing his cheeks, his breathing slow and even, and his features so familiar to her now, so completely mesmerising. Her fingers reached towards him, her heart fuller than it had ever been.

The subdued sudden ring tone of her mobile stayed her hand in mid-movement. As she realised what the sound was, she turned swiftly, crossing to the armoire in the corner of the room, where her handbag was contained. She whisked out her phone, set it to vibrate, not ring, and with a quick glance at Xavier to ensure he had not been disturbed by it hurried out onto the terrace, through the French windows that opened to the outdoors directly from the bedroom.

Nerves were strung like wires along every pathway in her body. Tension acute in every muscle.

It was Armand. She knew. It had to be.

And what he would tell her now, she could scarce bear to hear.

She clicked to receive the call.

Xavier awoke. For a second he did not know what had woken him, then he realised. A phone ringing. Muffled, cut off swiftly, but enough to rouse him, primed as he was to business calls at unsociable hours that suited others around the world better than they suited him.

He glanced around, locating his phone where it lay on the bedside table. He checked to see the display screen, but there was no message to indicate a missed call. His eyes moved around the room.

And saw Lissa outside, on the terrace, a bath towel wrapped around her, the sliding door imperfectly closed. She had her profile to him, her phone clutched to her ear. She was saying nothing, but her expression—

Shuttered, tight.

Tension netted him suddenly.

Who was calling her? Why?

And then suddenly her expression changed. He saw it happen in an instant. From shuttered to shining—radiant suddenly with delight, transformed.

She spoke. He heard her voice—muffled, but distinct.

'Oh, that's *wonderful!* I can't believe it! Are you sure? Are you really, really sure?'

She paused to hear the answer, and then she gave a laugh. A laugh of pure happiness. More than happiness.

'Armand—I'll love you for ever for this! I can't believe how happy I am. It's just so *wonderful!*'

She paused again, her face still radiant, still overjoyed. And

then her expression changed again. He could see it—see it with his own eyes. Her eyes widened, and wonder filled her face.

'Oh, Armand—is this true? Can you really mean that? *Marriage?* It's everything I could have dreamed of! Yes! Yes, of *course!* Of course I will. As soon as you want. Sooner!' She gave another laugh, happy and thrilled. Radiant with joy. 'Tell me everything. *Everything.*'

She began to wander away from the terrace, turning so that he could not see her anymore. Could not hear her.

But he did not need to see more. Hear more. He had seen and heard all he needed to. His eyes stared out into the room. There was no expression in them. None in his face.

But in his heart fury burned.

Implacable, unforgiving.

Deadly.

When Lissa came back into the bedroom, overcome with emotion, it was empty. Her heart was so full she thought she must burst. The call from Armand had been everything she had longed to hear. And so much more!

Her eyes lit.

Marriage—was that really, truly what Armand planned? But he had been adamant, determined. And she knew that to his proposal there could be only one answer. A thrill of happiness went through her.

On winged feet she dressed, relief and happiness soaring within her, then hurried out onto the terrace again, and around the corner of the house to gain the main terrace that opened from the living room. The table had already been laid for breakfast, and the scent of freshly brewed coffee, plus the heady aroma of croissants, greeted her enticingly. Xavier was not there yet, but she assumed he was making business calls, as he often did—pre-

ferring to get them out of the way early on, so they had more time to themselves during the day.

A pang went through her.

Xavier—

She would have to tell him.

Tell him why she must leave him.

For a moment she bowed her head, as if under the weight of too much emotion.

Armand, Xavier—

She took a breath. She would have to deal with it—she had no choice. It would be hard, but it must be done. And now at least she knew what Armand's plans were.

It made her own decisions so much easier.

She settled down at the table and reached for the jug of fresh orange juice. The housekeeper bustled out of the villa, checking that she had what she required. Lissa smiled and thanked her, as usual, for having set the breakfast out. The woman nodded and bustled away again, leaving Lissa to the tumult of her thoughts.

Where was Xavier? It was not fair not to tell him as soon as she could.

She gazed out over the vista in front of her, at the open grassy space bordered by tall pines, leading down to the sea, cobalt at this time of day.

So perfect, so beautiful.

Footsteps sounded behind her. She turned her head.

Her face stilled.

It was Xavier, as she had known it would be, but he was wearing not the familiar casual clothes he wore on the island but a formal business suit. Dismay filled her.

He had said he wasn't going back to Paris until the following day. She'd thought she had till then.

'Are we leaving *today?*' The words burst from her, anxious and dismayed.

He did not answer, merely took his place at the other end of the table from her. There was, Lissa realised, a closed look on his face. She watched him reach for the coffee and pour himself a cup. Absently, she noticed, with the familiar quiver that always accompanied her awareness of him, how the leanness of his wrist was accentuated by the sliver of gold watch strap, the pristine white of his cuffs, edged with the dark charcoal of his business jacket. She had always known how devastating he looked in formal attire, but now, seeing him again like this after two weeks of casual gear, he looked not just devastating but—formidable.

Distant.

'Xavier—what is it?'

She could not stop herself asking. Something had happened, and she could feel her chest tighten.

His eyes flicked up from setting back the coffee jug.

Something speared through her. It was like being impaled.

For a moment longer he said nothing, just let his dark, unreadable gaze rest on her. She felt a chill seep through her.

'Xavier—what's wrong?' Her voice was faint.

Did emotion flash briefly, searingly, in the dark depths of his eyes? She couldn't tell—his eyes were unreadable.

Abruptly, he spoke. His voice was as she had never heard it before.

'The launch will take you to Nice, and a flight will have been booked for you for London.'

'London? Today? But I thought…?' Lissa's voice trailed off.

A hollow was beginning to form in her stomach.

A dark eyebrow rose. His expression was suddenly saturnine. 'You thought? Ah, yes—you thought,' he repeated. He lifted the coffee cup and took a mouthful, setting it down again with a precise, controlled movement. Then, with the same precise, controlled movement, he rested his eyes on her.

There was no expression in them.

'Shall I tell you what you thought? It would be amusing, *non?* Because you certainly intended to amuse yourself. What is that expression in English? When the cat is away, the mouse will play?'

His eyes went on resting on her. Her face was expressionless.

Behind that studied, blank visage he knew what she would be doing. She would be thinking, thinking at breakneck speed—what to say, how to play it.

She had played it very well up to now. Superbly, in fact.

She had fooled him completely.

Rage, black and toxic, filled his lungs. He fought it back. This was not the moment for it. And she was not the only target.

He directed some at himself.

For being a fool.

A fool of such enormity that if he thought about it rationally, coolly, he would still be amazed by it. But amazement was not what he felt now. Now there was only a dark, savage rage inside him that had to be controlled or it would devour him. And he would not permit that. Would not give her the satisfaction of seeing it.

Let alone the other emotion he was feeling.

No, there was only one way to do this. With precise, absolute control.

His expressionless gaze watched her. There was an expression forming in her face now, in her eyes—those beautiful, lustrous eyes that had gazed into his so openly, so ardently…

No—that was not permitted. He sliced through his mind like a guillotine, cutting off the head of a corrupt, decadent aristocrat.

He watched the expression form.

Confusion.

Ah, so *that* was how she was going to play it. He waited for the words that would accompany the expression, and they came as he had known they would.

'Xavier—I don't understand. I don't understand what you are saying—what is happening?'

Her voice was strained, bewildered, anxious. All appropriate emotions to display in the circumstances. She was very good at displaying the appropriate emotions.

Such as passion, and desire…for him and him alone…

No!

The guillotine sliced down again. 'You don't understand?' he echoed sardonically. 'How can that be? You are returning to London. That is what you want, is it not? After all, you need to be safely back in your impoverished *atelier*, from which you will be swept away into a wonderful marriage with a handsome, rich young man.'

He watched as the expression of confusion deepened in her face. She opened her mouth to speak, but he forestalled her. His voice had the same deadly sardonic inflection as before.

'In fact, it is all arranged, is it not? Armand has proposed marriage to you, and it is *everything you ever dreamed of*, and you *will love him for ever* for it—*non?*'

Comprehension hollowed through her. He had heard her phone call.

'Xavier.' She spoke urgently. 'I can explain—'

A smile parted his lips. It chilled her to the core.

'Of course,' he agreed pleasantly. 'You will have at your disposal a very convincing explanation. Very probably a touching one, too. I expect you will explain to me that Armand is—what shall it be?—an old friend? A former lover still carrying a flame for you whose tender feelings you do not wish to hurt? Or perhaps he is someone in love with a friend of yours, and you are playing matchmaker? Who knows what else your fertile imagination will conjure up for my amusement? Perhaps I should even let you make the attempt now. But *hélas, le temps c'est pressant*, and I have a busy schedule to complete today. Commencing, of course, with your removal both from my life and…' he paused fractionally '…Armand's, as well.'

She could say nothing. Nothing at all. Only stare at him with horror and disbelief in her eyes. The savage fury bit again, and the guillotine's deadly blade sliced down once more.

'You did not really think,' he said softly, his eyes never leaving hers, 'that I would permit you to ruin my brother by marrying him, did you?'

A small sound escaped her, incoherent and strained. He ignored it. Ignored the expression in her eyes. Of course she would be horror-struck—at one blow all her dreams of a rich marriage were at an end. A rich marriage to a man on whom she had cheated even before the wedding could take place…with her bridegroom's own brother.

'Brother?' The word was scarcely audible.

He made a slight gesture with his hand.

'Yes, Armand is my brother,' he confirmed. His voice was light, still pleasant.

He watched her expression change again—more confusion and bewilderment, layered over the horror and shock.

'But…his surname is Becaud…'

He nodded acknowledgement. 'As is my stepfather's.'

'Your brother…' She echoed again, as if she still could not take it in. Then her face convulsed. 'But why?'

His eyebrows rose quizzically. 'Why did I seek an affair with you? To protect my brother—why else? When he told me of his intended folly, and my investigation of you revealed that you worked as a hostess in a place that was one step from a bordello, naturellement I took steps to protect him. I sought you out at the casino with that intent, and decided that the best way to remove you would be to seduce you myself. You were responsive to me, and that was all I required to effect my goal.' His voice changed minutely, then he controlled it again—because control was essential, imperative. 'It also served to confirm that my initial judgement of you was correct—you are unfit to marry my brother.

A woman who falls so rapidly into the bed of another man can have no feelings for Armand. Only—' his eyes glittered with a dark, malevolent light '—for his wealth. Tell me,' he went on, his tone conversational, his voice pleasant, with a deadliness in it that sliced like a razorblade, 'out of interest, how much have you taken him for already? Surely you have—but how much, I wonder?'

Her face seemed to blanch, and he knew with the same savage fury that he had hit home. The glitter in his eyes intensified.

'A considerable amount, I would venture. And tell me—again, out of interest—what touching fairy tale did you tell him to make him open his wallet on your behalf? A charitable cause that you support, perhaps? Or a sick relative in need of care? Or—?'

His voice was baiting, scornful. Annihilating.

A rasp from her throat silenced him. Her face was as white as whey, the skin stretched thin over her starkly outlined bones.

She got to her feet. The movement was jerky, like a puppet. A puppet whose strings were pulled too tight. For a moment something speared through Xavier that almost made him lurch up and go and catch her before she fell—catch her and hold her and embrace her and—

No! God almighty—had she not already fooled him so completely that if it had not been for the random chance of overhearing that damning conversation he might actually have gone on believing the fantasy he had woven about her? For the final time the blade of the guillotine crashed down. He would need it no more—she was revealed for what she was. Liar, cheat, treacherous, faithless, machinating… The list went on without end, without mercy or pity.

Destroying him.

But he would not be destroyed. He would not. Out of this destruction he would save one thing. Worthless, yes, but because it was all he could save he would. He spoke again, picking his words with deliberate intent.

'But my intervention on Armand's behalf has not been without its compensations.' His voice had changed again.

Lissa stared at him, her eyes distended, horror drowning through her. He started to walk towards her. She wanted to move, run, flee—she could not. She was grounded to the stone beneath her feet. He came up to her. She could catch the scent of his skin, feel the warmth of his body.

The dark glitter in his eyes.

He reached out to touch her. She could not move. He cupped her cheek, his fingers lifting the fall of her hair and stroked down the side of her face with languorous delicacy.

'You were very good in bed, *cherie*. Very good.' There was approval in his voice. Appreciation. 'I might actually have taken you with me.'

He smiled down at her, and sickness churned in her stomach.

'You know,' he said contemplatively, his fingers still warm on her skin, 'you could have done very well out of it. I would have been generous to you, *cherie*. Your lack of interest in spending my money was very convincing, very touching. It would have encouraged me to spend lavishly on you. But you still preferred the security of marriage, did you not? Yet my brother is nowhere near as rich as I am. Did you not realise that? No? Armand has money of his own, *evidement*, but it does not, *cherie,* compare to mine.' He paused a moment, eyes working over her face.

'I own XeL,' he said softly. 'Do you know how much that makes me worth?'

He told her, down to the last million euros, what his wealth was.

He saw the shock flare in her eyes, and savage satisfaction speared him. So she had not known. And now, of course, she realised just how much she had whistled down the wind. He put in one final twist of the knife.

'And, since you pleased me so very much in bed, *cherie,* who knows but I might have married you myself?'

He watched the emotion in her eyes, and the savage satisfaction came again.

'As it is—' he dropped his hand away and gave a light, careless shrug '—the comedy, such as it is, is ended.'

For a moment, his eyes changed again, a dark light at the back of them. His face tightened.

'Belle,' he murmured. *'Quelle dommage.'*

Then, as she stood frozen, immobile, sick, he reached for her once more, his fingers curving around her chin, tilting it upwards. He lowered his mouth to hers, slanting his lips. Effortlessly he opened her to him, tasting her in a leisurely, intimate fashion.

Then he stepped away. His face was a mask. His voice when he spoke was brisk, expressionless.

'You will return to London. You will inform Armand that you cannot, after all, marry him. You will do so by phone or letter. You will not meet him. I shall be keeping you under surveillance to ensure this, and if you attempt to meet him I will have you intercepted. For my brother's sake, to spare him any further distress after his mistaken hopes of love and marriage have been destroyed, I will not tell him of your affair with me. But—' he held up a hand '—if necessary I shall do so. Be in no doubt of that. I will not permit you to marry him. Do you understand?' His voice sharpened. 'Do you understand?' he repeated coldly.

Slowly she nodded. It seemed the only thing to do.

That, and keep herself upright, keep herself together, all the parts of her body—because she was falling apart, fracturing. Tiny hairline cracks were widening, breaking open, shattering her into a thousand pieces.

'Very well,' he said. 'And now—' he glanced at his watch '—you will leave. You have ten minutes to pack.'

He walked away, back into the villa.

Behind him, by the table, Lissa stood quite, quite motionless.

* * *

Time had stopped. She could see it flowing somewhere very far away, outside. She could see the wake churning behind her as the launch sped over the water towards the shore. She could see the shore, inching closer. So time must be moving, somewhere.

But not inside her. Inside her, time had stopped. Everything had stopped. She couldn't feel anything, couldn't do anything, couldn't think anything. Eventually, after a long time, the launch drew up at the quayside and the engines were cut, and someone was holding out a hand to help her out of the boat. Then there was a car, and she was sitting in the back of it, and it was nosing out of the marina onto the road, with other cars rushing back and forth, and people on the pavements, and shops and houses and buildings. And then the car was moving, and she was moving inside it, but nothing else was happening. The car reached the airport, and someone was ushering her inside, guiding her up to first-class check-in, and talking French over her head. And she was handing over her passport, and then she was going through into the departure lounge. Later—how much later she couldn't tell—she was sitting on a plane, in a first-class seat, and staring out of the porthole. The plane took off, and she felt her stomach lift and lurch and fall away like the ground below. The plane climbed up, up into the sky, sun dazzling in her eyes, and then it was heading north, inland, across France.

And as it flew time started again.

And with it came perfect recall.

Xavier walking out onto the terrace and shattering her into a thousand fractured, broken pieces.

Word by word she went over the revelations of the day.

Xavier was Armand's brother. He had sought her out. He had sought an affair with her deliberately, calculatedly.

To separate her from Armand.

With no other purpose.

Not chance, not desire, not anything other than cold, deliberate purpose.

Making everything, *everything* between them a lie. From the moment he had come into the casino—to the moment when he'd thrown her from him like a diseased carcass.

Hatred seared in her. What else could it be, the emotion that seared her flesh? Hatred for the man who had lied, and lied and lied to her—day after day, night after night—with every word, with every touch.

It was a glorious day in London, mocking her with golden sunshine. From the plane's window as it landed, and then from the long windows as she trudged along to baggage reclaim, she could see brilliant sunlight glancing off the parked planes and the airport buildings. Heathrow was crowded, thronged with people—busy, purposeful, hurrying. She walked through them like a dead person. Her suitcase was rotating slowly on the luggage carousel. Another hot wire went through her. It was not the suitcase she had set out from London with but a new one made from finest leather, presented to her in Paris, with her own shabby valise disposed of disdainfully. The distinctive XeL logo in gold lettering on the handles and edging leapt out at her.

XeL.

Xavier Lauran. X. L.

She had never noticed. Never realised.

But then she had never noticed that everything she had thought true about Xavier Lauran had been a lie.

It had been staring her in the face, and she had never realised.

I thought it was chance that brought him to the casino. I thought it was desire that made him want me. I thought—

She broke off. She must not think. That was forbidden to her now. Nor must she feel. That, above all, she must not do.

She hefted the suitcase off the carousel. Then she trudged

towards the customs exit to make her heavy, dead-footed way down into the Underground station. All around her, familiar English voices told her she was back in Britain.

On the train she sat in a near empty carriage, huddled in her seat like a wounded creature. Mortally wounded.

As she emerged into the glaring sunlight from the bleak South London tube station, the outer skin of her life slid back over Lissa like a glove she had scarcely removed. The unlovely streets of this poor district were still the same as they had always been. Her dingy flat had not changed, merely looked dingier than ever. The trains still rattled along a few yards from the rear windows, the curtains were still shabby, the mismatched furniture was still cheap and chipped.

It was as if she had never left.

There was one more task to be done before her old life closed over her again completely.

Dully, with leaden fingers, she got out her mobile. It would be early still in the States, but she could not help it. This was something she had to do. She had no choice. Xavier Lauran had given her none.

Slowly, heavily, she tapped out Armand's number.

Xavier was travelling.

Paris, Munich, Vienna. Then Hong Kong, Kuala Lumpur, Singapore, Manila. On to Australia, New Zealand. Back to Cape Town, Jo'burg, Nairobi, Cairo.

He did not stop. Did not pause. Three continents in three weeks before arriving back in Europe. And still he did not want to stop.

'He must needs go that the devil drives.'

Who had said that? He did not care. The devil was driving him. An army of devils, driving him on, on, with whips of red-hot wire. He worked—filled his mind with work, with business, with meetings and reports, figures and facts, surveys and budgets, plans

and forecasts. It did not matter what. It mattered only that he did not think, did not feel about anything except work, business.

He saw no one. No one outside those colleagues or business associates it was necessary to see. On his travels he lived in hotel rooms, accepting no invitations, going nowhere except on business.

He cut himself off from everyone outside his work. Friends, family—above all family.

He did not contact Armand. All communication with him in respect of XeL he left to others. Armand was in America still, and that was all that was important. That and the fact that Lissa Stephens had made no attempt to join him. His security reports on her—reduced to the briefest comment 'no movement beyond London'—assured him of that. What she was doing, so long as she was not with his brother, he did not care.

Would not care.

Because she had ceased to exist. Ceased as absolutely as if she never had existed. Had never sat beside him, looking like a cheap tart, while he deliberately lost money at the roulette table. Never stood in the rain on a wet London street, waiting for a bus he had deliberately made her miss. Never dined with him at a hotel for an evening he had deliberately engineered.

And never left that breathless, garbled message for him telling him that she was now free to have an affair with him.

Never made a fool of him—the fool to end fools.

His hands clenched, spasmed and painful. Forcibly he made them untense.

How had he let it happen? Let her make such a fool of him?

She had been so convincing. Letting him think that whatever had happened between her and Armand it was all over and she was free. Free to let him take her with him, to spend that time on the island—that false idyll that had, for her, merely been filling in time until Armand proposed to her.

He told me he would, and he did.

And she had accepted. Without a moment's hesitation or pause. Without the slightest sign of compunction or guilt that, even as she gave him her happy assent, her lover was in the bed she had just vacated.

Xavier's face contracted.

Bitch! Faithless to him—to me!

Faithless. Worthless.

Hatred of her seared through him. It had to be hatred. He would permit nothing else. Acknowledge nothing else. She had deceived and manipulated both himself and Armand, taking them both for fools. Faithless to both. Treacherous to both.

Yes, hatred was all he must feel for her.

Nothing else.

Lissa was keying sales figures and product prices into a spreadsheet. It required intense concentration to put the right data into the right fields, and she was glad of it. It kept her mind channelled, focussed. Occupied.

It was essential to keep her mind occupied. Busy. Full. Focussed. Every synapse that fired had to do so only on permitted topics. The work she was doing. The food she was buying. The cleaning she was doing. The book she was reading. The programme she was watching. The street she was walking along. Each activity taking up all her mind. Allowing nothing else in. Nothing at all.

Because if for a single moment, a single second, she failed to keep her mind occupied in such a way, it would arrive.

Memory. Bringing dreams that were even more of a lie than the reality had been. That were as false as Xavier Lauran had been.

How can I bear it?

The question sounded in her head—meaningless, pointless. She would bear it because she must.

She went on typing. Tap, tap, tap at the keyboard. Keeping focussed, keeping busy.

The subdued buzz of her mobile was scarcely audible. She had it turned down to the lowest setting, for the office she was currently working in did not like staff to use their mobiles on personal calls during working hours. But Lissa ignored that particular rule. She *needed* to have her phone on.

Hurriedly, she slipped the mobile out of her desk drawer, clicked it to silent, and slipped it into her sleeve. Then she got up and headed for the Ladies. As she gained the wash-basin area, memory scythed into her mind.

She had stood like this, at that insurance company, and phoned the number of XeL to get in touch with Xavier Lauran, to tell him that she was available for an affair with him after all.

Fool that she had been.

She took a breath, harsh and punishing, and crushed the memories away. Then she answered her phone. The tone had stopped, but it had been a text anyway. She opened it.

> *'Wedding this weekend all arranged. Air ticket to you by courier. A'*

She clicked off the phone. Savage satisfaction seared in her face. He had destroyed so much, Xavier Lauran, but this—*this* he could not destroy.

This at least was safe from him. And he could do nothing about it—nothing at all!

CHAPTER ELEVEN

XAVIER pulled at the seat belt straps in the helicopter, and fastened them with a swift movement. Then he nodded at the pilot and reached for his headphones, to silence the deafening roar of the rotors as the machine lifted off the ground at Nice airport. It was only a short hop, but every moment counted.

He had been in Seoul when the call had come through from his mother. She herself had been phoning from the Maldives, where she and Lucien, her husband, had been holidaying. She had sounded breathless, excited, and almost inaudible over the connection. But what she had told him had stopped him in his tracks.

'My darling, you must come home in time for it. It's completely out of the blue, and I could shake him for doing this. But Lucien and I will be on the next flight, and you must be, too. He says they'll be there for Saturday—can you manage that? Oh, it's so little time. I could shake him, I really could. To throw us like this at the last moment. I haven't even met the girl. And now he tells me the wedding is all arranged. How can it be? I have made no arrangements whatsoever. There are dozens of people to invite, but the wretched boy says he wants no one—just family. He says his bride wants a quiet wedding. But he doesn't say why. And, Xavier, darling, this is what worries me most—he says that although she may not be the ideal woman I would have wanted

for him, he loves her. What can he mean by that? What's wrong with her that I wouldn't want her to marry Armand? Oh, Xavier, darling boy, please be there in time—promise me you will.'

He had given her his promise.

Grimly, with a face as dark as night.

It was still dark.

The helicopter soared up over the azure waters of the Mediterranean, heading east towards Monte Carlo and beyond. Towards his mother and stepfather's house in Menton.

Let him be in time! Let him just be in time to stop it!

How had she slipped his guard? Met up with Armand? Had his security's surveillance operations grown sloppy over the weeks?

His face tightened. It didn't matter now—all that mattered was that he must reach his mother's house before his brother ruined his life by marrying a woman he must *not* marry.

Fury lashed him again. He should have told Armand the truth about her. Told him just what she was, what she had done. Warmed his own brother's bed.

Instead he had sought to spare Armand's feelings, relying on the threat he held over her head to stop her from trying to hold on to his brother.

Well, she had fooled him yet again, the treacherous little bitch.

I have to get there in time to stop it.

Only a personal confrontation would do, he knew. If he phoned, if he were not there to face her, she would find a way to get out of it. Find a way to convince Armand that black was white, that she was as pure as driven snow. Not a woman who had amused herself with his own brother while waiting for Armand to make his offer of marriage.

But *would* he be there in time? The outward flight from Seoul had been delayed, and he had had to change in Tokyo, and then again in Paris. He was cutting it fine—very fine. Mentally he urged the helicopter on. The coastline below was passing with

painful slowness. Villefranche, Monaco, Cap Martin, until finally Menton, and the Italian border just beyond. Landing in the grounds of his mother and stepfather's villa would be extremely tight, but it could be done. *Must* be done.

The old gold of the villa came into sight, its gardens terraced down to the sea. With skilled precision the pilot brought down the machine, cutting the rotors as soon as possible to minimise the damage to plants.

Xavier was out of the helicopter in moments, striding up towards the house. The terrace doors to the drawing room were wide open. He hurried his steps. A cluster of figures came to the French windows, drawn by the noise of the helicopter, which was now lifting off again.

He took in the group instantly. His stepfather Lucien, and his mother. A priest.

And Lissa.

Emotion punched through him. Overpowering, like a tidal wave. He strode up to them over the gravelled pathway.

Lissa was standing as still as a statue. Frozen. Emotion punched again.

She was wearing a frock. A floaty, floral frock, calf-length, like a ballerina, in palest ivory with printed flowers in soft yellows, and delicate sandals. She held a posy of flowers in her hands. Her long, loose hair was caught back in wings from either side of her face, a fresh flower at the clasp on the back of her head.

She looked impossibly beautiful.

Impossibly innocent.

Impossibly bridal.

His mother's face lit. 'Xavier! You came in time. Wonderful.'

She held her arms out to him, and perforce he had to drop a kiss on each scented cheek. She looked happy, radiantly so. Xavier's heart chilled.

She didn't know. But how could she? How could anyone? His

eyes seared Lissa—in all her beautiful, innocent, bridal beauty. How could anyone know the truth about her from the way she looked now?

Her face was expressionless. There was nothing in it. Savage fury blanked through him. Well, he would put some expression in it.

His stepfather Lucien was greeting him, introducing him to the robed priest. He answered automatically, his eyes skirting inside the drawing room for his brother. There was no sign of him. He stepped inside, and the others parted to let him in, then reformed.

'Where's Armand?'

Xavier's voice was curt.

'He'll be here.' His mother had answered. 'I know it's unusual, but—'

He cut across her. 'I have to speak to him. Alone,' he emphasised.

'Darling, I hardly think there's time.' His mother's voice sounded uncertain.

'Afterwards, my boy, afterwards,' agreed Lucien, nodding avuncularly.

Xavier turned on them. 'You don't understand. This marriage cannot take place.'

There was a gasp of consternation. But not from Lissa. She just went on standing there, her face expressionless.

Or was it? There was something in her eyes—something he would not identify. Something in the set of her jaw.

God, she was so beautiful!

No. The guillotine came down again with practised familiarity. He was not to look at her. Not to see her. Not to see the outward beauty that masked a nature that was without principle or scruple.

His stepfather was speaking. 'Xavier—what can you mean? It is all arranged. Short notice, I grant you, but—'

The priest was speaking, too. 'Monsieur Lauran, I do assure you everything is in order. I have dispensation to conduct the ceremony here because of the particular circumstances—'

Xavier cut across him, not listening. What the priest said was irrelevant. What his stepfather said was irrelevant.

'Armand can't marry this girl. It is out of the question!'

His mother's face took on an agitated expression. 'My darling, don't. This isn't like you. Yes, there are difficulties, of course, but—'

His hand slashed down. *Difficulties?* There are more than difficulties. There are impossibilities.' His eyes flashed around them all. He took a deep breath. This was going to be hard, punishingly hard, but it had to be done. He had to tell his parents, and his brother, just why Armand could not marry Lissa Stephens. It would be painful, embarrassing, distressing—but it had to be done.

'This marriage cannot take place,' he said flatly, 'for one overwhelming reason. A reason I will disclose to my brother.'

His eyes went to Lissa. She had paled, but she was looking very calm, very composed. Yet there was a shimmer of tension about her, like an aura. His gaze held hers. It was hard to make it do so, but he did it because he had to. He had emptied his eyes, to make it a tiny fraction easier.

Her gaze, too, was blank. Stonewalling him. Daring him.

Daring him to cause dissension in his family, to rend his relationship with his brother when he told him the truth about the woman he was on the point of marrying. Daring him to stop her.

He called her bluff.

'What do you think?' he asked, directing his speech to her. His voice was soft, deadly. 'Do you think this marriage should proceed? Do you think my brother's bride will make him happy?'

Now he was daring her—daring her to lie through her pearl-white teeth, and so condemn herself when he exposed the truth about her to his brother, his family.

She was speaking, and as she did his breath caught with the shamelessness of what she said.

'Yes,' she said. 'I think this will be a very happy marriage.'

Her voice was steady, composed. Her eyes held his. Unblinking, expressionless. Except deep in their recesses there was something…

He paid it no attention. Instead, his eyes narrowed. His voice was even more lethal as he spoke again.

'You think so? You think my brother will be happy, married to a bride who is nothing better than a—?'

The double doors to the hall beyond the drawing room opened suddenly. Xavier whipped around, his accusation broken off. And as he turned, he froze.

Armand was coming into the room. But slowly, very slowly. It was because he was holding out his arm to the figure beside him.

She was very slender, ethereally fair. She was wearing a long white dress, very simple in design, and her pale hair was loose, wreathed with a narrow band of blossom. One thin hand was resting on Armand's crooked arm, pressing down on it.

She walked haltingly, limpingly forward, dragging each leg, one step at a time.

She was very pretty, but her face was etched with lines of strain and pain. Intense concentration and effort sat in her eyes as one step at a time, Armand led her forward.

There was complete silence in the room.

Then, as if at an unspoken signal from Armand, his father lifted forward an armchair and his son guided the girl into it. She sank down, the stress ebbing from her face as the weight was taken from her legs. She looked up at Armand.

'I told you I would do it,' she said, her voice soft, low and intense. 'I told you I would walk to my own wedding.'

He smiled down fondly at her. 'And you did,' he said. 'And every day you will be stronger. Every day.'

An answering smile broke across her face, lightening the drawn look on her features. She broadened her smile to take in Armand's parents, the priest and Lissa. And then Xavier. Her

eyes widened. Armand followed her gaze and suddenly registered Xavier's presence there.

He surged forward. 'You made it! *Maman* said she wasn't sure you'd get here in time, but you did it. I knew you wouldn't let me down.'

He put his arm around his brother's shoulder. 'Come and meet her,' he said. 'Come and meet the woman I'm going to marry.' He led Xavier forward.

His feet trod numbly. His whole body was numb. His mind was numb.

Shock was detonating through him in slow, silent motion. His breath was stopped in his lungs.

Armand was speaking again. 'Lila, this is my big brother, Xavier. He likes to look after me—but he won't need to do so anymore, will he?' He threw an affectionate speaking glance at Xavier, then looked back to his bride again. 'Now I've got you to look after me, haven't I?' He looked again to Xavier, and swapped to French suddenly. 'This time you trusted me, Xav— and I thank you for it, from the bottom of my heart.' He switched back to English, his smile embracing both his bride and his brother. 'I am the happiest man in the world, Xav—and it's because of Lila.' His voice sounded constricted for a moment, then he recovered, stepping back.

'I'm sorry, I've just realised—Xav, there is someone else for you to meet.'

He turned around and held out an inviting hand.

'This is Lissa—Lila's sister. She looks after Lila the way you look after me, Xav. And she's been a fantastic sister—you don't know how much.' He took a deep breath. 'But let's leave all the talking until later. First...' His eyes went back to Lila and softened. 'First I have a bride to make my own.'

He took up a position beside the armchair, automatically taking Lila's hand. Then he looked at his brother.

'Will you stand beside me, Xavier?' he asked.

On stiff, frozen legs Xavier crossed to where Armand stood. And stood beside him. Beside his brother.

As he did so he realised that Lissa had slipped across to stand beside the bride. She stretched out a hand briefly, to touch the long, loose, fair hair, as if in benediction. Her ivory-coloured bridesmaid's dress was a perfect foil to the simple white bridal gown of her sister. Xavier could not look at her. Could do nothing. Think nothing. He saw his mother and stepfather move slightly closer together, their faces wreathed in smiles. The priest cleared his throat, stepping forward and producing from his cassock a prayer book. He paused a moment, and then, his eyes locking with those of the bridal couple, began the service.

'Dearly beloved, we are gathered today, here in the sight of God, to join together this man and this woman in Holy Matrimony—'

His sonorous voice sounded on. And still Xavier could do nothing. Think nothing. Nothing at all.

Because thoughts would not work. Not now. Not when the tide of emotion running in him was sweeping him away...so very, very far away. To a place he had never known existed.

The service was brief, a private ceremony for the bridal pair and family, but for Xavier it seemed to last for longer than he could endure. But endure it he must.

At the end of the service, as the priest pronounced the pair man and wife and his brother bent to kiss his bride—tenderly and lovingly, protectively and cherishingly—his mother and stepfather stepped forward. His mother stooped and placed her arms around her new daughter-in-law's frail figure.

'My dears, I am so happy for you both,' she said, and her voice sounded choked.

Then it was Lucien's turn. He bestowed a fatherly kiss upon

her brow. 'My son is a very fortunate man,' he said. His voice, too, was rich with emotion.

As for Armand and his bride—their faces held all that a newly married couple's should.

Xavier turned away. He could not look, could not watch.

When he turned, his eyes collided with Lissa's. A basilisk stare. Killing him.

As Armand's bride was welcomed into the family, Lissa came to stand in front of Xavier.

Deliberately she turned away from him, moving closer to Armand's parents and her sister. Armand was bending down, scooping up his bride. She lifted her arms around his neck, her expression radiantly happy. There was a general movement towards the doors. Lucien opened them and let Armand go through first, followed by his wife accompanied by the officiating priest. Then he stood aside for Xavier and Lissa.

Like mechanical automata they walked through. But as Lucien closed the doors behind them and joined his wife and the bridal pair as they went into the dining room for the wedding breakfast, Xavier's hand closed around Lissa's wrist.

'I must talk to you.'

His voice was as low as hers had been. But the emotion in it scorched like fire.

She turned to him. It was still the basilisk stare. Still killing.

'To tell me *what?*' she said. 'What can you *possibly* have left to say to me?'

His eyes flashed darkly. 'Why did you not tell me? Tell me the truth?'

She pulled her wrist away, as if his touch contaminated her. The wide hallway that stretched from the front entrance to another pair of doors, opening onto the gardens, was deserted. The wedding party had gone through into the dining room. Household staff were circulating. Xavier could hear the soft pop

of a champagne bottle being opened. Voices and murmured laughter. A mix of French and English.

He seized Lissa's wrist again, taking her by main force out of the house, onto the terrace. The warmth of the summer sun beat down upon their heads.

'Let me go!'

'I must talk to you. Why didn't you tell me the truth?'

A voice like snake venom hissed at him in return. 'The truth? You wouldn't know the truth if it bit you. Your twisted mind covered everything—you had it all worked out. Some filthy little casino hostess had got her gold-digging claws into your precious brother, and that was all you needed to know. All you bothered to find out.'

Xavier's face stiffened. 'My security team's investigations into who Armand was visiting only showed you living at that address—no one else was observed coming or going.'

'That's because my sister didn't come or go. She was in a wheelchair, trapped indoors for days at a time. The only time she ever went out was when I took her to the hospital for therapy.' The venom was still poisonous in her hissing voice.

'You were reported embracing my brother on the doorstep—'

Lissa's eyes flashed viciously. 'He was being *kind*. He knew how upset I was about Lila—he was trying to comfort me. He knew I was exhausted and in despair because it didn't matter how hard I worked—including at that vile job I had to take at the casino. And let me tell you something, Mr Oh-So-Bloody-Morally-Pure, there aren't many damn jobs you can do in the evenings that pay anything like the kind of money I had to try and put by. I'd have cleaned offices if I could, but the hostess job paid better, and I had to do it even if it meant I had to let creeps slime all over me and try and get me to do those disgusting private hires—' Her voice broke off, and she shook suddenly. Then she returned to her invective. It was pouring out of her, like bile from a wound that had never been staunched.

That never could be staunched.

'It didn't matter how hard I worked,' she repeated, the bitterness twisting in her voice. 'I did office work all day and that horrible casino work half the night, and I still couldn't get close to what I needed.'

'What do you mean? Why did you need to—'

He never finished the question. She yanked her hand away again.

'I've got nothing to say to you. *Nothing.* And now—' her chin lifted, her eyes flaring '—I'm going back indoors. This is my sister's wedding, and nothing is going to ruin it. I knew you'd be here, and I knew what you'd try and do—but I knew you'd never succeed. Armand doesn't care that his bride can barely walk, and he doesn't care that I was a casino hostess. So there's nothing you can do. Except go to hell. Just go to *hell!*'

CHAPTER TWELVE

SHE stormed off. Her heart was pounding. She'd known, just as she'd thrown at him now, that he would arrive in time for the wedding. In time to try and stop it. But she'd known he wouldn't succeed. Couldn't succeed. The love that bonded Lila and Armand was much, much too strong to be broken.

Her throat tightened as it did whenever she thought of Lila—and the miracle that Armand had wrought.

Xavier Lauran's falseness could not touch them.

And she would not let it touch her. Never again!

She was trembling with reaction, she knew. She'd been keyed-up ever since she'd arrived at the beautiful, imposing villa. Even though it was the setting for her sister's crowning happiness, for herself it could only be a place of torment. Returning her to memories that writhed like poison in her brain every time she looked out over the brilliant, azure sea towards the Îles de Lérins.

So close. A short boat ride would have taken her back there.

But they were as distant as the far side of the galaxy. On rapid clicking heels she walked down the wide, tiled hallway to seek the guest cloakroom. She needed to compose herself before joining the wedding party. She had to hide everything she felt about Xavier Lauran. To Armand, to his parents, they would never have met previously.

Ever since she had come back to London, with the destruction of everything she had thought true about Xavier lying in twisted, ugly shards at her feet, she had had to tread on eggshells when it came to Armand. She had known, above all, that she must not tell him what his brother had done—had only, instead, resorted to putting all her focus, all her emotion, into rejoicing at the miracle that had happened to her sister.

The miracle that she had prayed for. That the pioneering operation on her spine at the clinic in America where Armand had taken her would work, would undo the damage done in the car crash that had crippled Lila and killed her parents. Lila was all she had left, and her devotion to her was absolute.

As Armand's had proved.

It had been so hard to let him take Lila to America without her. She had longed to go with them, to give Lila the support and encouragement she had always given her these last, terrible two years since she'd been crippled. But she had let them go without her. Because she had seen the love she had so fervently hoped for spring between them. For hadn't Armand's eyes the very first time he'd seen Lila in her wheelchair by the hospital lift, lit with a light that had surely only meant he was instantly smitten? Lissa had known, when he'd taken her to America, that love was surely blossoming between them, and that because of that they needed no third person present. And Lila herself had been adamant, determined that she did not want Lissa with her during the treatment.

'Armand will tell you if the operation has worked—and it *will* work. I know it will. The next time you see me, Lissy,' she'd said, as they'd bade farewell at the airport, 'I want to be standing up—walking. I promise you I shall be walking. It will give me added resolve, knowing I've promised you.'

She had kept her promise. Lissa could feel tears start in the back of her eyes—familiar tears. Lila had indeed been standing

when Lissa had arrived at the villa to be the bridesmaid she had promised she would be—leaning on Armand's arm. And the tender, loving light in his eyes, the glow in Lila's, had told Lissa so much more than the brief phone calls and text messages from Armand, which had been all that had kept her going during the weeks gone by.

And now Lila would be happy—Armand, too—and nothing could spoil that.

Lissa emerged from the cloakroom, outwardly calm at least, and made her way into the dining room to join the wedding party seated around the large linen-covered table, covered in crystal, silver and napery, and decorated with exquisite floral arrangements. Her eyes avoided going to Xavier, who had already taken his place. Her place, she thanked heaven, was between Armand and his father. Xavier was between her sister and his mother.

She smiled around the table, murmuring about 'freshening up'. If her face was still flushed, she could not help it. Out of habit, her eyes went to her sister. But there was no need for the concern that had always been in her regard—and her heart glowed. Since she had joined her sister and Armand, here at his parents' house, Lissa had seen for herself the miraculous transformation in Lila.

Her throat tightened with emotion again.

Her sister had suffered so *much*—so much pain—held captive in her wheelchair, in the loss of hope that she would ever walk again.

The click of a knife on the edge of a glass interrupted her and quietened the general conversation around the table in which everyone was participating apart from herself and Xavier. She would not look in his direction, but she could tell he was not taking part—his distinctive tones were absent.

Out of nowhere, memory cut through her. She heard his voice as she had replayed it so often in the hellish weeks that had followed her return to London—his voice throwing at her all the

foul accusations that had shattered her like a hammer taken to a precious vase.

Her fingers tightened around the stem of the champagne flute that had been placed in front of her by one of the household staff as she'd taken her place at the table.

Now Armand was getting to his feet, holding his own champagne flute. He waited a moment, then glanced lovingly down at Lila, who was gazing up at him as though he were the sun itself.

'I want,' he said, speaking in English, 'to give a toast. To my adored bride—' the loving glance came again '—for making me the happiest of men. And to my parents, for welcoming her as their daughter. But I also want to toast a very special person.'

He shifted suddenly, and Lissa realised that he was addressing her.

'To my wonderful new *belle-soeur*. And she is, indeed, a "beautiful sister," not just in her own outward beauty—' he tilted his glass slightly in tribute '—but, and so much more importantly, in her inner beauty.'

Armand's eyes went to his parents, his brother.

'You know of the terrible tragedy that befell my bride's family—and my bride.' His voice had changed, was sombre. 'I will not dwell on it now, here in the brightness of today, but I will give a toast in spirit to the parents-in-law that I was destined so tragically never to know—and thank them from the bottom of my heart for their daughter, Lila, who was spared for me from the carnage that took her parents' lives. And thank them, too, for Lissa.' His voice changed again, sounding resolute now. 'Whose strength and fortitude and courage and determination did so much to support her sister in her terrible affliction and the injuries she suffered in that fateful car crash. Lissa—' he nodded at her, tilting his glass again as she sat there, a flush forming on her cheeks '—who worked day and night, never sparing herself, to put aside the money that was needed to pay for the specialist

operation in America that was her sister's only chance of escaping from the prison of her wheelchair.'

Armand's voice changed yet again, taking on a sombre note once more. 'It has been my immense privilege to have had the good fortune to be able to lift that crushing burden from her—to take Lila to America and make the operation possible and in so doing find my reward...' His eyes now went to Lila, sitting gazing up at him, lovelight in her thin, pain-etched face, and his voice warmed like the sun as he finished his speech. 'The dearest love of my life.' His free hand slid to his bride who took it in hers.

Holding Lila's hand, Armand raised his glass.

'To Lissa—'

She sat, head almost bowed, colour flaring along her cheekbones, as the others's voices echoed Armand's.

All but one.

She did not hear Xavier's voice.

She waited as Armand sat down again. Lila was reaching past Armand, her hand freed from his, and was squeezing Lissa's hand as it lay inert upon the damask tablecloth.

'The *best* of sisters.' Lila's low voice came, fervent with emotion, and Lissa felt her throat tighten again.

Then both Armand and his father were pressing their palms on her shoulders. Lucien was murmuring something reassuring in French, which she did not catch, and Armand's mother was beaming at her across the table. Then, with a little gesture to the staff, Madame Becaud signalled that the serving of the meal should begin.

For Lissa, the meal passed in a haze. She ate and drank mechanically, recognising that the food was exquisite, but unable to relish it. Memory intruded painfully—the memory of the last time she had eaten like this in France. Xavier's rustic villa on the Île Ste Marie might be simple in design and decor, a world away from this beautiful, gracious *belle époque* villa, with its lovingly

manicured gardens dropping in artful terraces down to the sea, but every meal there had been cooked and presented with the care and attention that was the pride of France.

She could not look towards Xavier. Yet as the meal progressed she heard his voice, speaking in conversation. Did it sound strained, tense? She didn't want to hear, didn't want to listen. Didn't want to know.

She only knew she would not let his malign presence spoil, for an instant, a second, her sister's happiness. A happiness that had come like a miracle—a miracle made possible by the incredible kindness and generosity of Armand. By his love and devotion to her. Armand had fallen in love with Lila, as Lissa had prayed he would do.

She felt again her heart squeeze.

Lila was happy and that was all that mattered. She would have given anything, everything, twice over for that happiness. Nothing else mattered.

She repeated it to herself until it ran like a constant refrain in the dark recesses of her mind.

Nothing else mattered. Only her sister's happiness.

Not hers.

Because hers, she knew, had been blighted for ever that day when Xavier Lauran had hurled his poison at her and shown himself to be a man for whom only one overwhelming emotion was possible.

Hatred.

Xavier ate, he drank, he made polite small talk with his mother, with the priest, with his stepfather, even with his brother and his bride. But about what he had no notion. For him, the wedding breakfast was a season in hell. He was inhabiting a parallel universe, a malign, unendurable universe, one in which everything he knew was wrong. And everything he did not know—had

not known—was like acid burning through his skin, etching into his flesh, his consciousness, a truth that was eating him alive.

His brother's bride was Lissa's sister. Not Lissa. Her sister. Who had been crippled in a car crash—a car crash that had killed their parents. Lissa had worked to support her—to earn money for the operation that would make her walk again.

Cold ran down his spine. Fingers of ice.

Words burned into his consciousness—words that were acid on his soul. The words he had thrown at Lissa that hideous morning.

He had to talk to her. Had to tell her.

The ice splintered in his spine. Tell her what? Tell her what she already knew—had known all the time?

Why hadn't she told him? Why hadn't she explained?

His expression tightened. He had to talk to her. Somehow. But how? When?

The endless meal was finally over. The priest got to his feet, taking his leave of the family. His mother and stepfather escorted him to a waiting car. Xavier was alone with his brother, and Lissa, and his new sister-in-law. Tension slammed through Xavier. Somehow he had to find a way to get Lissa away and in private. To his intense frustration, she was sticking like glue to her sister, hovering over her as she remained seated in the bridal chair. Then Armand was there.

'Lila must rest a little,' he said, coming protectively to stand behind her, placing his hands on her frail shoulders. She turned and smiled up at him.

'No—please. I'm not too tired,' she told her brand-new husband.

But Armand shook his head. 'You know what the clinic said— a little exertion every day, no more. After being immobile so long, you must build your strength again little by little. And besides—' he dropped a kiss on her head '—I want you rested this afternoon so that you will look as beautiful as an angel for the party tonight.'

He threw a glance at Xavier. '*Maman* contented herself with

this private ceremony, Xav, but nothing on earth could prevent her pulling out all the stops for a grand party this evening. Even with such short notice as we gave her she has found a remarkable number of people to attend. So I want Lila fully rested in good time.'

He came around and with a fluid movement scooped Lila up into his arms. Lissa hovered at his side.

'I'll help you to your room,' she said.

But Lila shook her head. 'Darling Lissy—you don't have to do that anymore. I've got Armand now.' A glance was exchanged between her and her bridegroom, familiar and intimate, enclosing themselves in the privacy of the newly wed.

Then Armand spoke. 'Xav, why don't you show Lissa around? *Maman* will be plaguing the staff in preparation for this evening, and *Papa* will have hidden himself away in the library for a nap while she fusses. So make good your escape and show Lissa the gardens. They're beautiful, and the views from the gazebo are wonderful.'

'Thank you.' Lissa's voice was stiff. As stiff as frozen metal. 'But I think I might rest in my room, actually.'

Her hand was caught, and Lila was tugging her gently but inexorably closer.

'No, Lissy, do go with Xavier. Armand thinks he needs to relax. He had a punishing journey to get here in time, because we gave his family so little notice of our wedding plans, and he's a terrible workaholic, Armand says. If he doesn't take you around the gardens he'll just go and get sucked into his laptop. So do go off with him. Besides...' Her voice dropped with conspiratorial humour. 'He's so absolutely, gorgeously good-looking, isn't he? And you've never looked lovelier, Lissy.' Lila's pressure on her fingers squeezed tight suddenly. 'Oh, Lissy, I can't believe how happy I am. I just can't believe it.' Then she dropped her sister's hand. 'Now, off you go.' Her eyes were sparkling.

'Yes—go, *go*,' echoed Armand. 'And, no, you do not need to check your e-mails, Xav. XeL will survive an hour longer without your attention. Go on, take Lissa round the gardens.'

Xavier was beside Lissa in an instant. He could feel her stiffen. Feel her revulsion coming at him. He didn't care. He had to talk to her. *Had* to.

'*Mademoiselle?*' he said formally, indicating the French windows opening onto the gardens. Perforce, Lissa stepped through onto the terrace beyond.

Lila giggled. 'Lissa—not *mademoiselle*. We're all family now.' She laughed as she was borne away by Armand.

The moment they were gone, Lissa rounded on him.

'I'm going nowhere with you.'

Xavier's face hardened. 'Do you want your sister upset, today of all days? Have consideration for her feelings instead of indulging yours.'

The sheer effrontery of his admonishment took Lissa's breath away. But his hand was closing around her elbow. It might look as if he were merely guiding her along the path, but the iron grip burned on her skin.

He walked her down the cascade of steps that led through the terraced gardens. So brief a while ago he had raced up here, with no thought in his mind other than preventing the marriage of his brother.

Now the universe he had been living in had become a completely different one. Urgency impelled his steps.

I have to talk to her.

It was all he could focus on.

He got them down to the gazebo, a pretty little stone-built folly that afforded privacy, as well as views and shade and a sea breeze. The moment she could, Lissa broke away from his grip and went and sat at the far side of the gazebo, on the stone bench that ran around the interior. He rounded on her instantly.

'Why didn't you tell me? That's all you had to do. Tell me the truth.' It was all he could think about. It blotted out everything else. 'Why did you let me say those things to you? Why didn't you hurl them back in my face?' His voice was vehement, eyes dark and stormy.

In return, baleful eyes glared at him, her face stark and stretched.

'Why should I have? Like I said, your twisted mind had it all worked out. Worked out so well you wouldn't have believed an alternative explanation if it had landed on your head with a twelve-ton weight. And in case you've forgotten I *did* try to explain to you. But you just sneered and said that *of course* I'd have an explanation—a very touching one, you said. And then, when you demanded to know if I'd already succeeding in parting Armand from his money, I knew—' She gave a harsh, bitter choke of laughter, cut off immediately. 'I knew that it would be impossible for me to justify myself. Because Armand *had* already spent his money on Lila—she was already in America and he'd already paid for the operation and all the care she had to have at the clinic afterwards. So there was no chance at all of clearing my name.'

He was staring at her.

'I don't believe this. I don't believe you are saying this. Good God, how can you possibly think that I would have continued to think badly of you if you'd told me what Armand's money was being spent on?' He shook his head heavily. 'Do you really think me so low?'

She said nothing, and Xavier felt a knife slide into him. Then another one as she spoke again.

'You said I would come up with some fairy tale—"a sick relative in need of care" was one suggestion.' She quoted the words that had writhed in her memory ever since.

He blanched. 'But your sister *did* need care. She existed. She was real.'

'And you really would have allowed your brother to spe

kind of money on her? To actually marry her? You told *me* I was a gold-digger—why not Lila? Go on—why not? And she was worse than a gold-digger—she was a cripple, as well. Hardly an ideal bride.'

In Xavier's mind he saw the words of Armand's e-mail to him—the one that had announced he had found the woman of his dreams.

I know there will be problems, but I don't care if she isn't the ideal bride you think I should have…

His blood ran cold as he realised, now, why Armand had said what he had. In a harsh, bleak voice, he said again, 'Do you really think me so low that I would object to your sister because of her injuries?'

'It was what they were both worried about—and not just you, but Armand's parents, as well.'

'And did my mother and stepfather react with hostility?' Xavier demanded. His eyes bored into Lissa's.

'No,' she said, her chin lifting. 'They have been…' her voice worked '…wonderful. They have welcomed her like a daughter.'

'As I welcome her as a sister—my brother's bride.' He spelt out each word. 'God Almighty, how monstrous would I be not to do so?'

His eyes lasered hers, and she felt their force drilling through her. 'Do you know how I felt when your sister came into the room? When everything I held to be true, *knew* to be true, turned upside down? When I realised just how devastatingly wrong I had been?'

'I hope it hurt. I hope it damn well crucified you.' Lissa's voice lashed like a whip.

His mouth was a thin line. 'Your hopes are well founded,' he said. 'And you may also know how much worse I felt when my brother told us of how you had tried to earn the money to pay

for Lila's operation yourself. What you were prepared to put yourself through for your sister's sake. And yet again I ask you— *why* did you not tell me why you were in that sordid job? Do you think I would have condemned you if I'd known why you worked there? So why, *why* did you never tell me?' There was accusation in his voice.

Lissa's eyes widened disbelievingly.

'Tell you? What business was it of yours?'

A French expletive broke from him.

'What business was it of mine?' he echoed. 'We spent two weeks together. Do you not think that enough to let me know something, *anything,* of the truth about you?'

She backed away from him, horrorstruck. Disbelieving.

'Truth?' It was her turn to echo him now. 'Truth—you speak to me of truth? You complete and absolute bastard. How dare you say that to me? How dare you? The only truth I ever got out of you was when you threw me out. *Then* I got the truth. I got the truth about what you'd done to me.'

She shut her eyes, unable to bear this. Unable to bear the horror of it.

'You boasted of it,' she said. 'You boasted of how you had deliberately sought me out in order to seduce me away from Armand. You boasted of it—and then you threw me out like I was some kind of filth.'

Her eyes had flown open again as she hurled her accusation at him. She saw him blanch, and a savage gladness filled her. Darkness misted her eyes, her mind. The darkness of rage.

And worse, much worse.

'It wasn't like that.' His voice was flat.

'Yes, it *was!* You told me—to my face. You told me exactly what you'd done. Sought me out and seduced me—cold-bloodedly, calculatingly, deliberately. Your only purpose was to make sure I couldn't ever trap your brother into marriage.'

'No.' His denial was immediate, urgent. 'No, Lissa—listen to me. *Listen*. It wasn't like that.'

'You mean you *didn't* deliberately seek me out in the casino?'

His teeth gritted. 'Yes, yes—I did that. But—'

'So it is true, then, isn't it? Everything you hurled at me that morning on the island. Everything.'

'No.'

Her eyes flashed fire. 'You've just admitted it. You've just said it was true. You deliberately sought me out, deliberately singled me out for your attention. Because you thought I was some kind of slut who wasn't fit to marry your brother.'

'I didn't think that—I needed to find out, that was all. Lissa, listen to me—I was justified in being suspicious on behalf of my brother. He's too trusting, too…gullible. He's been taken in before—by a woman who preyed on his good nature, took advantage of his kindness and generosity. When he told me he'd met someone he wanted to marry, I had to protect him. I had to make sure that this time he was not being targeted by another unscrupulous gold-digger who was just after his money. That's why I had you investigated. I needed to find out what kind of woman Armand was involved with. I had to check you out—personally.'

'And remove me from being any kind of threat to your brother.' Her voice was flat now, her face dead. 'By seducing me. In cold blood. Just to be on the safe side. Because I was obviously, as a casino hostess, unfit to marry into your family.'

He breathed in sharply. 'It wasn't like that.'

She lost it again. 'You keep saying that. You keep saying it like some kind of parrot. "It wasn't like that. It wasn't like that." But it was. And you've admitted it. So don't even try and deny it. Because there's no point.'

She dragged air into her ragged lungs, harshly and tearingly. When she spoke again it was with a defeated, deflated air.

'And there's no point talking anymore. I accept—all right? I accept what you've told me. You didn't know. You just didn't know. I never told you about Lila and you're not a mind-reader, so how could you possibly know about her? All you saw was a woman who worked as a casino hostess and was apparently having an affair with Armand simply because he was a rich guy and I·was after his money. You knew your brother had told you he wanted to marry a girl you thought was me, so you moved in to protect your brother—how the hell can I blame you for that? And how can I blame you for misinterpreting that phone call from Armand and assuming it was *me* he was talking about marrying—not Lila? And when you heard me blithely accepting, even though I'd just been merrily having a fling with another man, it just confirmed, in your eyes, that Armand meant nothing to me. I can't blame you for thinking that.' She took another harsh breath in.

'I can't blame you for anything,' she said bleakly. 'Anything at all. The whole thing was just…just…a screw-up, that's all. A screw-up.'

She turned away, pressing her hands down over the low balustrade that girdled the gazebo. Bougainvillaea rioted over the stonework and climbed up the gazebo supports, brilliant crimson. A butterfly hovered over one of the vivid blossoms, then fluttered away to sip another flower, the pattern on its wings in complete focus. Everything was in super-focus. Crystal-clear.

Just like what she now knew about what had happened to her.

A screw-up. No other word for it.

Heaviness crushed her. She'd wanted to hate Xavier for what he'd done to her, but how could she? He hadn't treated her badly because it hadn't been *her,* the real her, he'd manipulated and accused. He'd done it to some mythical gold-digging floozy who had never existed.

The butterfly was still sipping its nectar. Then it stretched out

its wings again. The pattern wasn't in focus any more. It was blurred. And getting more blurred with every second. She ought to go indoors. There was no point being here. She straightened her shoulders, lifting her chin, blinked to clear her vision. Then she turned.

Xavier was still there, watching her.

Her stomach hollowed at the sight of him. The way it always did—every time she saw him. She quelled it immediately. No point in that. None at all. What did it matter that Xavier Lauran stood there, turning her knees to jelly? What did it matter that he'd once held her in his arms, kissed her, embraced her, made love to her so breathtakingly that the universe had burned for her? Of course it didn't matter. It hadn't mattered for weeks now—not since that morning when he'd explained just why it was that he'd had an affair with her. Deliberately, calculatedly, cold-bloodedly. To separate her from the brother he'd assumed she was trying to ensnare into marriage.

So why, if it hadn't mattered for weeks now, did it feel as if a knife were being plunged into her side? Slowly, and with exquisite intent to hurt her.

She knew the answer. Because until this moment she'd been using her hatred for him for another purpose.

Anaesthetic.

Crude, but effective. Effective enough to make her capable of functioning. To get through the weeks, the days, the endless hours. Make her capable of enduring seeing Xavier again here, like this, at her sister's wedding.

But she'd had to let go of the hatred. She couldn't blame him for what he had done. End of story. End of hatred.

But if the hatred went, what would be left?

The knife in her side reached deeper. Closer to its target.

Her heart.

Terrifying realisation swept through her. Without her hatred

for Xavier Lauran only one thing was left. And it damned her, damned her utterly.

She would have to go. As soon as possible. Tomorrow. Tonight she had to stay for the party that Armand's parents were giving for the bridal couple—she could not leave before then. But tomorrow she would leave immediately.

And until then she would just have to get through. Endure.

She lifted her chin. Xavier was looking at her, but there was nothing in his face. Nothing in his eyes. That was good.

'So,' she said, 'that's that. It was all just a screw-up. That's all.'

Something shifted in his eyes.

'That's all?'

'Yes.'

He walked towards her. There was something very controlled in the way he was walking. She took a step back, but she was already against the stone balustrade.

'You call everything that happened between us a screw-up?' There was nothing in his voice beyond measured enquiry.

'Xavier, I've just said I can't blame you for what you did. You wanted to protect your brother and that seemed the best way to do it. That's all there is to it.'

'You think that, do you?' The same measured tones. They made her angry suddenly.

'You said yourself that's how it was. You said yourself that was the truth of it. You spelt it out with crystal clarity that morning. Just because you didn't know I wasn't who you thought I was, it doesn't stop it being the truth of why you had an affair with me. To free your brother from me and for no other reason.'

The knife slid in deeper as she made herself say it. It was the truth—brutal and cruel. But it didn't stop it being true. However much it hurt.

There was something in the back of his eyes, but she didn't want to look. Didn't want to meet his eyes. She wanted to get

away. But the stone balustrade was preventing her. Her hands pressed back against the stonework as if she could push it away.

He was standing in front of her. Far, far too close. Her breath was tightening in her lungs.

'And what about this truth?' he said. His voice changed. Husked. Her palms pressed down onto the stone as if she would collapse without it.

His hands reached for her, cupping her face.

'What about this truth?' he asked again.

What had been at the back of his eyes was at the fore now. She could see it, and it made her tremble. It was liquid gold, and it was pouring from him and melting through her.

He lowered his face to hers. His kiss was slow, and deep and sensual. It melted down her spine. But she mustn't melt. She must not. It was essential she did not melt. Ever again.

She pulled away. 'This was *never* the truth. It was just a lie to protect Armand from me.'

'Don't you understand?' he demanded explosively. '*That* was the lie. Telling you that I'd had an affair with you in order to separate you from my brother. *That* was the lie. Because it was the only way to hit back at you for what you'd done to me—betrayed, as I believed, everything I'd believed we had between us. It was never true, Lissa, *never.* Yes, I sought you out at the casino deliberately. But once I'd seen you for yourself, I wanted you. It was torment to think of you as being my brother's intended bride—and when you contacted me to tell me, so I thought, that your relationship with Armand was finished, I snatched you to me. I shut everything out of my mind, until…until that morning, when my world imploded around me. Hearing that call, thinking you were returning to marry Armand after all, nearly destroyed me. Forgive me, I beg of you, for what I said to you then. For all that I thought of you so wrongly.'

She swallowed. Her throat hurt. Her body hurt. Everywhere in her whole being hurt.

'On the evidence you had, it was reasonable to think what you did,' she said. What else could she say?

'Reasonable?' he echoed. His voice sounded hollow. 'Yes, you are right—it was very reasonable of me to think what I did.'

There was a strange look in his face.

'Reason. Logic. Evidence. Truth. Good words. All of them. Every one of them.' His voice had changed—it seemed to come from very far away. 'They were the words I used about you, Lissa. Right from the start—when I first heard of your existence and looked at that damning photo of you—and right to the end. When I heard your conversation with Armand and damned you with it. I applied reason to every judgement I made of you— every decision I took about you. It's the way I've lived my life— with my head. Always my head. Always logical—always rational. Nothing else ever made sense to me.'

He took a breath—deep and rasping.

'But you see…' he said, in that same strange, remote voice, that came from somewhere so very far away. And she stood there, unable to move, unable to think or breathe. 'You see, there was something I omitted to take into account in my dealings with you, Lissa. Something I must tell you—something I have discovered.'

He paused, and when he spoke again his eyes were very clear, his voice very clear.

'I've always trusted reason,' he said, 'but it does not answer everything. You see…' his clear, clear eyes held hers '…*le coeur a ses raisons, que la raison ne connaît point.*'

For a long, timeless moment she held still, letting the words enter her mind.

'Do you need me to translate?' His voice was quiet, his eyes, so clear, still holding hers.

She shook her head. His face was blurring. She could not speak. Only whisper. *'The heart has its reasons, which reason does not know.'*

She felt the tears well up in her eyes, well and spill like diamonds. Her face constricted.

He was there in an instant. She reached gropingly for his hands. The warmth of his fingers enclosed hers. Safe, cherishing.

She felt her heart turn slowly over.

'Xavier—' It was a breath. A hope. A hope she dared not have.

He folded her hands against the strong wall of his chest. She could feel the heavy beat of his heart. He was so close to her, so close.

He gazed down at her. His eyes were dark, and they stayed the breath in her lungs.

'My heart, Lissa—my heart is yours. And it is what I should have trusted all along. Not what I knew, but what I felt.'

The tears ran down her cheeks. Washing away so much— so much pain and hurt. He kissed them away, his lips tender. And then his mouth sought hers again, and into his kiss he poured his heart.

'Ah, *mignonne*, how much I love you.'

She clung to him. She was weeping now, and he held her, cradled her and murmured to her, cherishing her and keeping her safe. As he would for ever.

Emotion swelled in him like a wave. Gently he drew her down to sit on the stone balustrade. For a long while they sat, while Lissa quietened, and then they sat longer still, content to wind their arms around each other and gaze out over the azure sea beyond.

Presently, she spoke.

'I tried to hate you, Xavier—or what you said to me, for what you did to me—but it only covered up what I truly felt. It hurt so much, knowing that everything I'd thought was between us was just a lie—that you had planned and manoeuvred and plotted the whole thing. That everything was false. Everything you had done or said—except during that last hideous exchange—was false.' She took a ragged, shuddering breath. 'Because to me—

to me it had been the most precious time of my life, those weeks with you. I didn't think it could last—I never dreamt that you could love me. I only knew that I had taken that time with you, while Lila was in America, and that if the operation had not worked, if Armand hadn't felt for her what I'd so hoped, so prayed he did, then I would need to go to her, to be there for her. I could not abandon her to chase my own happiness. I did not dare love you…'

She lifted his hand, still holding hers, to her mouth.

'But Lila has her miracle—and her miracle is not just her escape from the prison of her wheelchair. It is Armand. As mine…' her voice wavered '…as mine is you.'

She kissed his hand again, and folded it to her, then reached to kiss his mouth.

Love was in her lips.

Her gaze.

And happiness such as she could not believe was in her heart, and in her soul.

He cupped her cheek and smiled at her.

'I would marry you this minute, this hour, this very day. I love you so much, *mignonne*. But let us give your sister and my brother their celebration together—we will not steal their thunder. We will dance at their wedding, and they—' he smiled again '—they will dance at ours. But I cannot wait until then, *mon amour,* to make you mine again.'

He nodded down towards the base of the gardens. 'My step-father keeps a launch at the villa's private mooring, just below. We do not need to put in an appearance again here for quite a few hours. So I was thinking—'

Lissa looked at him.

'It's a fast launch,' said Xavier. 'It would get us back in time for the party tonight.'

'Back from where?'

But she knew. Knew exactly where Xavier wanted to take her.
And where she longed to go.

He drew her to her feet. His eyes were glinting suddenly, and
just as suddenly her knees were as weak as jelly.

'Where we found our happiness,' he told her. 'And where,' he
said, 'we'll have our honeymoon.' He frowned momently. 'Are
you content with such a simple destination? My villa on the Île
Ste Marie? Or do you want to go somewhere else?'

She shook her head. 'I only want you,' she said. 'Wherever
in the world you are.'

'And I you. All my life.'

He pressed a kiss upon her mouth to seal their vow, and then,
with mutual, unspoken haste, they headed down to the sea, and
to their life and their love together.

THE ROYAL HOUSE OF NIROLI

Always passionate, always proud.

**The richest royal family in the world—
a family united by blood and passion,
torn apart by deceit and desire.**

By royal decree, Harlequin Presents is delighted to bring you
The Royal House of Niroli. Step into the glamorous, enticing
world of the Nirolian Royal Family. The ailing king must find
an heir…each month an exciting new installment follows
the epic search for the true Nirolian king. Eight heirs, eight
passionate romances, eight fantastic stories!

BRIDE BY ROYAL APPOINTMENT
by Raye Morgan
Book #2691

Elena is drawn to Adam—the illegitimate child of a
Nirolian prince—and his little son, who's in need of
a mother….But for Adam to marry her, he must put
aside his royal revenge.

*Don't miss the final installment of this fabulous
series, when the true heir shall be crowned!*

Coming in February:
A ROYAL BRIDE AT THE SHEIKH'S COMMAND
by Penny Jordan Book #2699

www.eHarlequin.com

HP12691

REQUEST YOUR FREE BOOKS!

2 FREE NOVELS PLUS 2 FREE GIFTS!

PASSION GUARANTEED SEDUCTION

YES! Please send me 2 FREE Harlequin Presents® novels and my 2 FREE gifts. After receiving them, if I don't wish to receive any more books, I can return the shipping statement marked "cancel." If I don't cancel, I will receive 6 brand-new novels every month and be billed just $3.80 per book in the U.S., or $4.47 per book in Canada, plus 25¢ shipping and handling per book and applicable taxes, if any*. That's a savings of close to 15% off the cover price! I understand that accepting the 2 free books and gifts places me under no obligation to buy anything. I can always return a shipment and cancel at any time. Even if I never buy another book from Harlequin, the two free books and gifts are mine to keep forever.

106 HDN EEXK 306 HDN EEXV

Name	(PLEASE PRINT)	
Address		Apt. #
City	State/Prov.	Zip/Postal Code

Signature (if under 18, a parent or guardian must sign)

Mail to the **Harlequin Reader Service®**:
IN U.S.A.: P.O. Box 1867, Buffalo, NY 14240-1867
IN CANADA: P.O. Box 609, Fort Erie, Ontario L2A 5X3

Not valid to current Harlequin Presents subscribers.

Want to try two free books from another line?
Call 1-800-873-8635 or visit www.morefreebooks.com.

* Terms and prices subject to change without notice. NY residents add applicable sales tax. Canadian residents will be charged applicable provincial taxes and GST. This offer is limited to one order per household. All orders subject to approval. Credit or debit balances in a customer's account(s) may be offset by any other outstanding balance owed by or to the customer. Please allow 4 to 6 weeks for delivery.

Your Privacy: Harlequin is committed to protecting your privacy. Our Privacy Policy is available online at www.eHarlequin.com or upon request from the Reader Service. From time to time we make our lists of customers available to reputable firms who may have a product or service of interest to you. If you would prefer we not share your name and address, please check here. ☐

HP07

HARLEQUIN *Presents*

*The Rich, the Ruthless
and the Really Handsome*

How far will they go to win their wives?

A trilogy by Lynne Graham

Prince Rashad of Bakhar, heir to a desert kingdom,
Leonidas Pallis, scion of one of Greece's leading dynasties
and Sergio Torrente, an impossibly charismatic,
self-made Italian billionaire.

Three men blessed with power, wealth and looks—
what more can they need? Wives, that's what…and
they'll use whatever means to take them!

THE DESERT SHEIKH'S
CAPTIVE WIFE
by Lynne Graham
Book #2692

Rashad, Crown Prince of Bakhar, was blackmailing Tilda over
a huge family debt—by insisting she become his concubine!
But one tiny slipup from Rashad bound them together forever….

Read Leonidas's story in

THE GREEK TYCOON'S DEFIANT BRIDE
by Lynne Graham
Book #2700
Available next month!

www.eHarlequin.com

HP12692

HARLEQUIN Presents

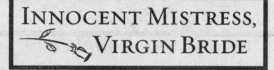

INNOCENT MISTRESS, VIRGIN BRIDE

Wedded and bedded for the very first time

Classic romances from your favorite
Harlequin Presents authors

Harriet Flint turns to smolderingly sexy Roan Zandros
for a marriage of perfect convenience. But her new
Greek husband expects a wedding night to remember…
and to claim his inexperienced bride!

Meet the next Innocent Mistress, Virgin Bride
in February 08:

ONE NIGHT IN HIS BED
by **Christina Hollis**
Book #2706

www.eHarlequin.com   HP12696

Men who can't be tamed...or so they think!

If you love strong, commanding men—
you'll love this brand-new miniseries.

Meet the guy who breaks the rules to get exactly
what he wants, because he is...

HARD-EDGED & HANDSOME
He's impossible to resist....

RICH & RAKISH
He's got everything and needs nobody....
Until he meets one woman...

RUTHLESS
In his pursuit of passion; in his world the winner takes all!

THE ITALIAN BILLIONAIRE'S RUTHLESS REVENGE
by Jacqueline Baird
Book #2693

Guido Barberi hasn't set eyes on his ex-wife since she left him.
He will have revenge by making her his mistress....
Can she resist his campaign of seduction?

If you love a darkly gorgeous hero,
look out for more Ruthless books, coming soon!

Brought to you by your favorite Harlequin Presents authors!

www.eHarlequin.com

HP12693